TERROR MOUNTAIN
GERRY GRIFFITHS

SEVERED PRESS
HOBART TASMANIA

TERROR MOUNTAIN

Copyright © 2018 Gerry Griffiths
Copyright © 2018 by Severed Press

WWW.SEVEREDPRESS.COM

All rights reserved. No part of this book may be reproduced or transmitted in any form or by any electronic or mechanical means, including photocopying, recording or by any information and retrieval system, without the written permission of the publisher and author, except where permitted by law. This novel is a work of fiction. Names, characters, places and incidents are the product of the author's imagination, or are used fictitiously. Any resemblance to actual events, locales or persons, living or dead, is purely coincidental.

ISBN: 978-1-925711-84-4

All rights reserved.

DEDICATION
For my brother, Steve
A mountain man in his own rights

1

When Ray Pike got the call from Josie Mills that her husband, Lewis, had gone after a large predator that had broken into their stockade and slaughtered some of their goats, Ray didn't even hesitate. He grabbed his keys off the peg by the front door and shambled out to his truck as fast as he could.

At 67, and with arthritic hips, Ray hoped to spot his friend from the road, as he wasn't in any condition to go traipsing through the woods. Maybe Lewis could flush the murderous heathen his way and Ray could pick it off from his truck.

He sped down the rural road; the worn tires on his old Dodge pickup kicking up dirt and gravel under the chassis. Driving with one hand on the big steering wheel, he reached up to the gun rack hanging across the rear window of the cab, grabbed his varmint rifle, and laid the weapon on the bench seat.

He'd been in such a hurry to rush out the door and come to the aid of his friend that he hadn't thought to grab an extra box of .308-caliber shells from the dresser by the front door.

Keeping his eyes on the road, he leaned over and dropped the door on the glove compartment, hoping to spot an ammo box inside, but there was nothing but the truck registration and some tattered maps.

He ejected the four-round clip while he drove and was relieved to see that the magazine was full, knowing he would have been as worthless as a wooden nickel showing up with a gun without any bullets.

He saw Josie standing on the side of the road at the end of the Mills' driveway. She was holding a single-barrel shotgun. When Ray took his foot off the accelerator to slow down, she pointed firmly down the road, and yelled for him to keep going. He could see that she was mad, as she prized her livestock, but at the same time he swore he saw a look of fear in her eyes.

Josie Mills was a strong woman, a hard-working farmer's wife, and had performed every husbandry chore imaginable from assisting duress animals giving birth to having to make the tough decision when an aging animal could no longer get up on its own and was in too much pain.

Ray knew whatever Josie had seen, it had to have been terrible.

He waved and kept going, following the windy road through the mountainous forest.

He cranked his window down. He couldn't hear anything, but the sound of the laboring engine so he slowed down and stopped. "Lewis!" he yelled. "Can you hear me?" he continued to shout.

"Over here!" a voice answered not too far off.

Ray gazed through the dense trees and saw a swath of orange. Lewis must have slipped on his hunting vest when he'd grabbed his gun so he could be easily spotted in the woods. He'd known Ray would come a running—which was now only a figure of speech—when Josie called and said they were in trouble.

But then Ray had second thoughts, and instead of remaining in the truck, he figured he'd be more useful going out to meet Lewis, bad hips or not. He reached inside his shirt pocket and grabbed the tiny packet of aspirins. He ripped off the corner, shook the tablets into his mouth, and crunched them up.

Whenever his joints would flare up, he'd pop some aspirins, and always carried a packet or two with him at all times. It generally helped to dull the pain. Lately his gut had become a bubbling lava pit from all the aspirins he'd been taking. It had gotten so bad some mornings, he was spitting up blood in the sink.

He opened the truck door, grabbed his rifle, and scooted down off the seat. He felt a sharp twinge of pain in both hips the second his boots hit the ground. He took a deep breath and shut the door.

He'd parked near the edge of the road, which dropped off about five hundred feet down into the gorge where the Diamondback River flowed between its rocky banks like a sidewinder traveling down through the mountainous terrain.

Walking with noticeable limps, he headed into the trees where he soon found Lewis waiting anxiously. "I think it went this way. The ground's so hard, I can't say for sure."

"Any idea what it is?" Ray asked, pulling back the bolt on his rifle, and sliding a cartridge into the chamber.

"My guess, it's a wolf—and it's a big one. Bloodthirsty bastard ripped our goats to shreds. Looked like they'd been run over by a harvester and churned up in the blades. Never seen Josie so upset."

"Did you call Avery?" Ray asked, thinking they could use the sheriff's help.

"Not until I know what we're dealing with," Lewis said. He was five years younger than Ray with the same sinewy build, but unlike Ray, Lewis had the energy and endurance of a man ten years his junior. He'd brought his .12 gauge Browning pump.

"Which way do you think it went?" Ray asked, squinting up at the trees stretching up into the forest.

"Probably hightailed it up the mountain," Lewis replied.

The two men stood quietly and listened for a moment. Ray gazed up, drawn by melodious sparrows perched in a Douglas fir.

Then abruptly, the birds stopped singing.

A twig snapped behind a nearby covert of high brush.

Ray and Lewis turned in the direction of the sound.

"Shit, Ray," Lewis said, giving his friend a worried look. "Damn thing doubled back."

"Ah hell," Ray yelled as something huge charged out of the thicket. The blinding fury roared and cuffed Ray alongside the head. Sharp nails raked the right side of his face like a hot knife cutting through a soft stick of butter. Blood gushed into his eyes and down his neck. A powerful blow drove into his sternum and sent him sprawling on his back in the pine needle covered dirt.

Ray could feel the ground tremble. He gazed up through the crimson veil and saw a massive foot come down and stave in his ribcage.

"Son of a bitch!" Lewis hollered and fired his shotgun.

The retort was so loud Ray flinched. He felt like he'd been knocked down and run over by a bull.

There weren't enough aspirins in the world to make this pain go away.

Ray attempted to raise his right hand to wipe the blood out of his face but the second he moved his arm, a sharp pain shot up his forearm and into his elbow.

Lewis must have scared the animal off because he was pulling Ray up off the ground.

Ray let out a pitiful moan when Lewis tried to raise his injured arm.

"Sorry, Ray." Lewis switched around to the other side and lifted Ray's left arm up so that he could drape it over his shoulder, grabbing onto Ray's left wrist.

"What the hell was that thing?" Ray groaned. Before Lewis could answer, they'd taken a step and Ray screamed with pain.

"I know you're hurting but we've got to get to the truck," Lewis said.

Ray whimpered with each hobbling step.

"Hang in there, Ray."

"I can't...just leave me," Ray moaned, unable to endure the pain, knowing that any second he was going to black out.

"Just a little bit farther," Lewis coaxed. "We're almost there."

Ray couldn't even move his legs and Lewis had to drag him but it didn't matter because by then they had reached the back of the pickup. Lewis managed to unhook the tailgate and drop it down. He had to shove an old tire and some remnants of firewood out of the way. He grabbed Ray around the chest and hefted him up onto the metal bed.

"Don't you worry, Ray."

Ray could hear Lewis' footsteps as he ran up to the driver side and opened the door. Lewis started the engine and turned the truck around.

As the vehicle gradually picked up speed, the stiff ride in the back became bumpier and each jarring shock made Ray cry out. He grabbed the railing of the truck bed and tried to sit up to tell Lewis to slow down. He raised his head and saw the huge beast in pursuit. He fell back just as the enormous creature vaulted up into the back of the truck.

"Oh, God..." Ray screamed.

He wailed as the thing ripped into him.

His world suddenly became a kilter when the truck spun off the road and flipped over on its side, tossing Ray out into the great beyond. The truck rolled over his mutilated body and continued to tumble all the way like a pinecone plunging down the precipice, crashing on the boulders at the bottom of the deep ravine.

The creature stood on the edge of the road. It took a moment and stared at the twisted wreckage down below then stepped back and stomped off into the forest.

After a moment of dead silence, the song sparrows began singing again.

2

Marcus Pike drove his 1990 Ford F-150 up the dirt strip and stopped the truck a few feet away from the porch steps of the farmhouse and shut off the engine.

"Well, what do you think?" he asked Libby, sitting stoically on the passenger side. He could tell by her expression his wife wasn't duly impressed.

He couldn't really blame her.

The place was rundown in need of repairs and looked abandoned like it hadn't been occupied for years instead of only being vacated for a three-month period since his grandfather's tragic accident.

A rotted board on the second step of the riser leading up to the porch was cracked in half in the middle and had probably snapped under someone's weight. A post was missing leaving a gap in the porch railing. The siding on the front of the structure was gray and weathered and needed to be painted. Sections of the wood shake roof were missing shingles. A deflated tire on a rusted rim and a wheelbarrow missing a handle were heaped with some other junk visible in a tall clump of weeds by the trees.

Shortly after attending his grandfather's closed-casket funeral—at the strong advice of the mortician—Marcus received a call from a trust attorney that there was a last will and testament and that Ray Pike had left his estate to his last immediate living relative, his grandson, Marcus, as Marcus' parents had both died in a traffic accident five years ago.

There had been just enough money in the old man's savings account to take care of his funeral arrangements but he had thought enough of his grandson to leave him the farm on the three-acre parcel.

"We moved out of our apartment for this?" Libby frowned, shaking her head.

"Don't be so quick to judge. I know it needs work but it's ours," Marcus said.

"This place looks yucky," seven-year-old Kaylee griped from the jump seat in the extended cab.

"Right now it does," Marcus said, "but we'll fix it up."

"I want to go home," Kaylee said.

"This *is* our home." Marcus turned around in his seat and smiled at his daughter. "Remember the story I used to read to you when you were little; the one about the snail that had to crawl all the way across the backyard so it could be with its family?" referring to a popup book he used to read to her before bedtime.

"Because the boy raked him up and dumped him in a pile of leaves."

"That's the one. And how it took the snail so long to get across the yard. What did you learn from that story?"

"That snails are slow?"

"No, Kaylee. *Patience*. The snail knew if it persisted, no matter how long it took, it would eventually reach its family."

"What your father is trying to say," Libby interceded, "is that things take time and little by little before you know it, we could make this place look like home."

"Really?" Marcus gave Libby a dubious look. By her immediate reaction when seeing the farmhouse for the first time he had suspected she would continue to resist their move to the country.

"Well, we're here now," Libby said resignedly, nodding over her shoulder at all their luggage and belongings piled up to the ceiling inside the camper shell.

"Okay, then." Marcus clapped his hands and rubbed his palms together. "Let's take the grand tour!"

They got out of the truck and stretched. The six-hour drive from the city had been long and tedious, even though they had taken the opportunity to refuel on the way and pulled off a couple times for potty breaks at the roadside rest stops.

Marcus glanced around the property.

A split rail fence had collapsed that edged alongside the barn several yards away from the rear of the farmhouse. Nearby was a dilapidated chicken coop constructed with a hob nosh of different building materials: interior doors and sheets of plywood and various-colored fiberglass typically used for patio covers. The poorly built enclosure was fenced in with an assortment of remnant poultry netting that looked like discarded end pieces. It was evident that his grandfather saw more importance in functionality then esthetics.

A section of a small pen where Marcus remembered his grandfather kept a handful of goats and sheep was leaning at an extreme angle and on the verge of toppling over.

Marcus had never thought of his grandfather as being a lazy man. There were times as a kid whenever he visited, the two of them would go on long walks in the woods or hike down steep trails to the river and fish. Back then, everything had been well kept up and there had been plenty of farm animals.

It saddened Marcus to see the place in such disrepair. He figured the farm had become too much for his grandfather to maintain as he got older and the place slowly declined. Marcus felt bad that he had not kept in touch with his grandfather in the past ten years. He knew his grandfather was too proud to ask for help. Marcus wondered if he would have dropped everything if he *had* called. Or would he have found an excuse not to come, as he was too busy with his own life being married and raising Kaylee?

"Marcus, do you have the key?" Libby and Kaylee were already on the porch, cupping their hands over their brows and staring through the windows to see inside. He'd been so distracted he hadn't noticed they'd gone up on the porch.

When he came over, he noticed that Libby had proactively taken a short plank from a strewn pile of wooden posts and boards by the lattice skirting around the base of the porch and placed it across the broken step.

Marcus climbed up the steps. He reached inside his jean pocket and dug out the small set of keys that had been given to him by the attorney. He chose a key that looked like a match for the front door but when he went to insert it into the lock, he found that the door hadn't been locked, as it slowly swung inward as soon as he touched the knob.

"You don't think someone broke in?" was Libby's first suspicion.

"Maybe it was never locked. I doubt neighbors out here worry much about crime like they do in the city."

"Even so, you don't want people just walking in."

"Okay. Let me go in first and take a look. If everything looks normal, I'll call you both in." Marcus glanced down and saw the worried look on Kaylee's face as she stared up at him. He gave her a reassuring smile and winked, then pushed the door open and stepped inside.

It was plain to see that his grandfather hadn't been much of a housekeeper by all the clutter and mess in the front room. Even though it was sunny outside, the interior of the farmhouse was gloomy and didn't reflect much light as the walls were covered with dark brown panels. It was like stepping into a cave.

A dresser that should have been in a bedroom was next to the door. Marcus saw a drawer that had been pulled out and not pushed back in. Inside were packages of fishhooks and red-white bobbers.

A fly rod and half a dozen fishing poles were leaning against the piece of furniture. Marcus recognized one of the fishing poles he had used as a kid. Seeing it still there made him sad that he hadn't spent more time with his grandfather.

A worn checkered plaid armchair and a matching tattered couch faced the stone hearth. The coffee table in front of the settee had a broken leg; most likely from all the fishing and outdoors magazines piled on the tabletop. He looked down at the hardwood floor. The surface was scuffed and there were places where the planks had warped from the damp and lifted up.

He did a quick walkthrough and checked the kitchen facing the rear yard then went into both bedrooms downstairs, but didn't find anything that would suggest that anyone had come in to rob the place. He went up the narrow staircase that led to the landing of the loft. Again, there were no signs of intruders.

Marcus came back down and walked over to the front door and opened it all the way. "It's okay to come in."

Libby held Kaylee's hand and they came inside. Libby took a moment and gazed about the room. "This is a little rough."

"Nothing a little TLC won't cure," Marcus said, trying to liven the mood.

"It's like a tomb in here."

"Definitely need to repaint these walls. What do you think? Some cleanup, furniture covers, I could sand and refinish the floor? Might look pretty nice."

"I don't know, Marcus. This looks like a lot of work."

"And when have you been afraid of rolling up your sleeves?"

"It's just..."

"Mommy, can we go see the barn?" Kaylee asked.

"Sure, let's go check out the barn," Marcus said thankful for the diversion and grabbed his daughter's hand.

"You guys go ahead," Libby said. "I need a few minutes."

"Careful," Marcus hollered after Kaylee as she ran ahead and rushed down the rickety porch steps.

Marcus followed Kaylee around the edge of the farmhouse and caught up to her before she could dash through the open doorway of the barn. "Wait up, you don't want to run in there and step on something sharp."

"I've never been in a barn before," Kaylee said excitedly.

Like the farmhouse, the barn needed a lot of work. One of the large doors in the front had broken off the hinges and was lying on the ground.

"Ooh, what's that smell?" Kaylee said, pinching her nose.

"That's what a barn smells like." Marcus took a deep breath. "I bet you can't identify each smell."

"Like what?"

"Well, can you smell the hay over there?" Marcus pointed inside at one of the stalls.

Kaylee looked at him suspiciously then slowly removed her hand from her face. She inhaled through her nose. "Yeah, I can."

"If you close your eyes I bet you can smell the animals that were in here. Grandpa used to have pigs and goats and sheep. Do you smell them?"

"I smell poop."

Marcus laughed. "I bet you do. Why don't you go back to the house and see if Mom needs you to help her unpack?"

"Okay." Kaylee spun on her heels and raced back to the farmhouse.

Marcus stepped into the tenebrous barn. He looked up at the rafters and noticed a few bird nests. A wooden ladder stretched up to the hayloft. He walked by one of the support beams and smacked the wood like he was kicking the tire of a car he might be considering. The structure seemed sound enough.

An old tractor was tucked in the back of the barn, partially covered by a rotted tarpaulin. There was a plow and some other discarded farm equipment next to a few hay bales.

Marcus walked by a workbench where his grandfather kept most of his tools, hammers, screwdrivers and handsaws hanging on a pegboard. Shovels, pickaxes, a posthole digger, and a pitchfork were leaning up against the wall. Shelves stocked with cans of paint and wood stains that had accumulated throughout the years.

He counted four stalls, two with gates. As he got closer to the back of the barn he noticed sunlight shining onto the ground from behind a partition. He could smell a foul odor, which made him want to gag. "What the hell is that?"

He stepped around the other side of the partition and found a rear door leading into the barn that had been left open. Here was another stall. The hay was flattened down, like something big had slept on the bedding. Marcus crouched and sifted his fingers through the smelly straw and found loose berries and skeletal bones of what he believed to be trout.

He squished a berry between his fingers and red juice squirted out which meant that it wasn't very long ago that something had been camping out in the barn.

Marcus thought it best to keep his discovery to himself, at least for now. No point in giving Libby anymore reason to question his decision uprooting the family.

Tomorrow, he would board up the rear door and dissuade the squatter from getting in.

3

Ever since they arrived at the campsite near the Diamondback River, Cole Wagner couldn't shake the feeling that they were being watched. Maybe he was just tired. The five-hour eight-mile hike over and down the mountain had been extremely arduous, as they had to haul in both their camping and prospecting equipment plus enough food to last them a week. Besides their heavy backpacks, Cole had lugged a four-foot sluice box while his wife, Kate, had carried a couple of white five-gallon buckets by the handles, one tucked inside the other.

The spot was right on the shore at a bend where a tributary split off into a creek from the larger body of water and was the perfect spot for setting up the sluice box and panning for gold.

No sooner had they dumped their packs on the ground, Cole insisted they set up the two-person dome tent and collect firewood for a fire later before they started prospecting.

Cole spent most of the afternoon out in the creek while Kate worked the nearby bedrock on a hill. He had set up the sluice box far enough into the stream to capitalize on the fast moving water but shallow enough that he could stand in his knee-high waterproof rubber boots and not get his socks wet. He'd used the standard rule of thumb and angled the gradient at a one-inch drop per each foot-length of the sluice box and had placed a heavy cobblestone on the aluminum contraption to weigh it down so it wouldn't get swept away by the swift current.

Using a garden trowel, he scooped the last of the earth out of the bucket he'd balanced on some rocks and slowly shook the dirt and gravel into the dump box. He watched through the metal grate as the water passed over the manifold and carried the loose material over the first riffle then dropped more sediment on the second riffle depositing the finer material. Once he'd picked out the stones and debris, he removed the cobblestone, and lifted up the lightweight sluice box.

He unsnapped the riffle tray and pulled out the expanded metal screen. After removing the rubber carpet trapping the retention material, he rolled it up then stood the sluice box up inside the bucket. He rinsed the residue from the carpet. Making sure that there wasn't any precious metal left behind, Cole scooped water from the creek and drizzled it down the smooth aluminum surface until he was satisfied that he had cleaned off the sluice box and everything had accumulated at the bottom of the bucket.

He was anxious to take a break after standing out in the creek for hours but wanted to sift through this last load of material. He removed the sluice box from the bucket and placed it on the rocks, weighing it down with the cobblestone so that it wouldn't take off and float downstream.

Cole grabbed his green plastic 15-inch gold pan that was resting on the rocks and poured in the contents from the bucket. It was mostly a mix of sand granules and clay. He wedged the pail between two boulders, and then holding the pan with both hands, he dipped an edge into the water and filled it halfway. With the pan still underwater, he began shaking it back and forth so that the lighter material would float out. He kept sloshing out the unwanted particles until there was only black sediment remaining in the bottom of the pan.

A smile came over his face when he spotted color around the edges of the pan. He was hoping for a small nugget but he was happy with the gold flecks. Leaving just a little water in the pan, he unsnapped his shirt pocket and took out his gold guzzler bottle, which had a two-inch tube on the end. He put the tip of the tube over a gold fleck, siphoned it into the bottle then sucked up the other flecks in the same fashion. Afterward, he carefully transferred the yellow flecks into a vial, which when full, the gold would weigh approximately one gram, maybe more.

With the current gold price at $1,330 per troy ounce—equating to 31 gold vials—it was indeed a tedious process but worth the return if they discovered a high-concentrate placer.

Cole grabbed the sluice box and bucket and waded ashore. He placed everything on the gravelly ground and rolled down his wader boots just above the ankles so it would be easier to walk around on dry land.

He looked beyond their campsite and saw Kate ten feet up on an embankment of bedrock. She was using a folding pick shovel to dig out material and dumping it in her bucket. The hillside was a series of striations of metamorphic and sedimentary rock from millions of years of glaciers wedging a path through the gorge and the weather's constant erosion.

Cole called out to Kate but she didn't hear him as she was wearing a set of earbuds and listening to her MP3 player hooked on her belt. He had to wave his arms to get her attention. When she saw that he was taking a rest she stuffed the short spade into the bucket and carried it back with her to the campsite.

"Any luck?" Kate asked, removing her earbuds and letting the cord dangle behind her neck. She dropped the pail next to a log by the fire pit.

Cole took the glass gold vial out of his shirt pocket and held it up between his thumb and forefinger. The gold glittered in the sunlight.

"Not bad."

"Oh, and I suppose you did better?" Cole said even though it wasn't a competition. Whatever they found would be shared jointly.

Kate directed Cole's attention to the 14-inch pan on the blue tarp in front of the tent. He walked over and saw seven decent-sized gold nuggets in the colander. The smallest was the size of a peanut, the biggest one almost an inch across at its widest point. Each nugget was flat, like a gob of yellow Play-Doh scraped off the bottom of a shoe. He was staring at more than an ounce maybe close to two ounces of placer gold.

"Holy shit, Kate!"

"Holy shit is right," Kate beamed.

Cole gathered up the nuggets and deposited them into a small cloth bag and cinched up the tie. He went into the tent and stuffed the sack into a side pouch on his backpack.

"Pretty good for the first day, wouldn't you say?"

"Super, but the day's not over," Cole said, eager to get back to prospecting. "We've still got another two hours of daylight left."

"You want to eat something first? I'm starving."

"Sure. How about some Top Ramen?"

"Fine by me."

Cole set up the single burner camp stove attached to a portable propane canister and fired up the burner while Kate poured some water into a pot and ripped open a packet of dried noodles. She shook the clump into the pot and handed it to Cole who set it over the flame.

While they sat on the log and waited for the water to boil, Cole noticed a sign lying on the ground behind them with a bunch of crumpled Olympia beer cans. "Where was that?"

"Someone had tossed it in the bushes."

"Damn." Cole had posted the warning sign, which read "NO TRESSPASSING OF MINERAL RIGHTS" against Kate's better judgment as she thought it wasn't wise to advertise but he thought it would dissuade people from going on their mining claim.

Obviously, he'd been wrong.

Even though he and Kate had the sole mineral rights and had recorded their claim with the county clerk's office and the U.S. Bureau of Land Management, they didn't own the property being that it was public land and anyone could campout or fish the stream; or in this case, party and leave their beer cans.

Who the hell hikes five hours to get drunk with their buddies?

"It's almost ready," Kate said. She tore open the seasoning packet and dumped the powder into the boiling pot of water.

After another minute, Cole attached a snap-on handle to the pot and poured the noodles evenly into two metal cups.

He hadn't realized how hungry he was until he started smelling the aroma steaming off his cup. Kate handed him a spoon to stir his noodles. He blew on the hot broth and took a sip, warming his insides.

After finishing his noodles, Cole got up and walked over to the stream to rinse out his cup.

"What do you think, should we both work the bedrock?" Kate asked, joining him and dipping her empty mug in the water.

"You know, it's probably our best bet, but I'd still like to try around the bend."

"Why? My spot's better."

"Maybe so, but..."

"Then go. Freeze your dumb butt off," Kate said and dismissed Cole by splashing him with the droplets still left in her cup.

"Tomorrow," Cole said, sensing Kate's irritation. Even though he knew she was right and their chances of finding gold were better in the bedrock, he still wanted to pursue panning the creek. They were both stubborn and would occasionally butt heads on an issue. This was probably no different. It wasn't a matter of being right or wrong; it was getting to eventually win the discussion, something that Cole rarely did. "We'll tackle it together later. I promise." Even a compromise could feel like putting a point on the scoreboard.

"Just be back before dark," Kate said.

"Yes, Capitan." Cole leaned in and gave Kate a kiss.

"When you get back you can make us a fire."

"I thought you were already hot and bothered."

"Try and not to fall in."

"I'll do my best." Cole grabbed his bucket by the handle making sure the trowel was inside and placed his gold pan on the rim. He started down the shoreline and glanced over his shoulder. Kate had popped her earbuds in and was carrying her shovel and bucket back over to the area of bedrock she'd been working.

Cole never really considered himself a conservationist, though he did take pride knowing he wasn't leaving carbon footprints wherever he went. When they had first started mining their claim they promised each other that they wouldn't destroy the natural beauty of the outdoors by ruining the terrain and tearing up the land prospecting for gold, which was another reason he preferred panning in the water as it was less detrimental to the environment.

As he walked across the rocks he got that nagging feeling again that he was being watched. He stopped and looked across the creek at the opposite bank. Beyond the water's edge was a small meadow then a towering wall of junipers and pines. He stared at the trees, thinking that any moment something was going to jump out at him.

But nothing did.

Cole continued on and made his way along the rocks to where the creek elbowed at a junction. He gazed out at a large rock in the middle of the crystal clear stream. The swift current had created a pocket in front of the boulder that was on the edge of a slight step that sloped another 12 inches down below the surface.

The cup near the base of the boulder was the ideal spot for finding gold. As gold was generally six times heavier than other minerals, there was a good chance there was some of the precious ore trapped deep in the pocket.

Cole leaned down and rolled his waders back up to his knees. Even though the creek was moving rapidly, he wasn't too concerned as the water in the middle wasn't more than two feet deep; three feet where the bottom dropped down but he had no intention of going that far downstream. He studied the uneven bottom for the best path and stepped into the surging water. He kept his legs far enough apart so he wouldn't get swept off his feet.

Making his way over to the boulder, he rested his right knee against the rock and leaned down to survey the depression. He was right in his assumption, as there was plenty of sediment deposited in the hollow. Using his trowel, he began to dig out the loose material and fill his bucket.

He stepped around the backside of the boulder to get a better angle.

His right boot slipped on the slick, underwater rocks. He immediately grabbed the boulder with both hands to steady himself but his weight and his backward momentum caused the large rock to shift on the ledge...

Pinning the top of his boot.

He tried pulling his foot out of the rubber boot, but it was wedged tight.

Cole still had the trowel in his hand so he crouched and started digging at the base of the boulder to free his boot. But then he stopped when he realized he was undercutting the heavy rock and it would crush his leg if it were to roll down on him.

He was in a serious world of shit.

"Kate! Can you hear me?" he yelled.

He continued to call out her name and plea for help but there was no reply.

He doubted if she could hear him over the running water no matter how loud he shouted especially if she was wearing her earbuds. He wondered if she knew he had drowned while she was listening to her music if that particular sound track would forever play in her head and haunt her for the rest of her life.

No need to panic, he told himself.

But it wasn't until the sweat began to drip down his brow and his pounding heart threatened to punch out of his chest that he realized how scared he really was. He yanked and yanked like a madman but his boot wouldn't come out. He gave it one big tug hoping that would do the trick...

And fell back into the water. He went under the surface, striking his head on the rocky bottom.

He flailed his arms and bent his free leg back to push himself up but the current was too strong and forced him back down.

He gulped for air and got a mouthful of water.

It was impossible to get any leverage with his boot jammed under the boulder.

Every time he tried to raise his head out of the water and sit up, his hands would slip on the slimy rocks and the power of the water would shove him back under.

His oxygen-deprived lungs were on fire.

What a shitty-ass way to die, he cursed himself. He lay motionless on the bottom and gazed up from his watery grave.

A dark shadow loomed above him.

No doubt his inept guardian angel late for their appointment.

4

Sheriff Avery Anderson pulled over and parked his Ford Bronco on the side of the dirt road at the edge of the forest. He could hear the river rumbling through the gorge out his half-opened window. He left his hat on the passenger seat and climbed out.

There was no one around, just him. Once a day he'd come by this way. Check on Josie's memorial. Like it was his duly appointed job to make sure no one tampered with it. Seemed the least he could do being that Lewis and Ray had been his best friends, more like brothers through the years.

Josie had nailed a large silver cross to the trunk—a new addition—the kind most god-fearing folks tacked on their bedroom wall above the head of their bed. A yellow ribbon was draped around the base of the tree, securing a white vase filled with long stem white roses and yellow daisies; flowers freshly cut from Josie's garden. Tucked in a bowl under the vase was a snapshot of the two men, much younger, standing next to a split rail fence they had built together, each with a boot on the lower railing, proud as could be.

Three months passed, and the poor woman still grieved for her Lewis.

Avery ambled over and gazed down into the deep canyon. He could see patches of the Diamondback River through the trees below as well as the brown hunk of metal crumpled on the rocks five hundred feet down. After a rescue team from the U.S. Forest Service had rappelled down the cliff and claimed the bodies of Lewis Mills and Ray Pike, it was decided there was no point in recovering Ray's pickup as it was completely totaled and wasn't worth the time and spit to haul it up.

He turned and started back to his truck. A cool wind blew through the nearby trees and he looked up at the mass of dark clouds grouping in the north hinting that a storm might be approaching. He hadn't heard anything forecasted over the weather broadcast and didn't see any reason for concern. Even if a cold front did move in, the first storm of the season was usually nothing more than a few light flurries, and whatever did stick to the ground, would be melted away by late morning.

Before opening the door to his truck, Avery glanced up the road to the entrance to the Mills' driveway.

He'd been up to visit Josie a few times after the accident, drinking coffee in her kitchen. Reminiscing about Josie's husband and Ray Pike until it became too much for him to bear, sitting across the table, wanting to share his feelings for Josie but not knowing when would be the right time. He could tell she still pined for Lewis, and understandably so. Lewis had been a striking man, rugged-looking from working the farm, handsome even in his 60s.

Avery knew he could never have competed with Lewis. Even though he tried to stay in shape, his physique had suffered from his sedentary lifestyle sitting behind a desk in his office and grabbing quick bites behind the wheel whenever he went out on a call. There were nights he would respond to one emergency after another which meant going out unshaven and without a shower, sometimes wearing the same wrinkled uniform for two days.

Certainly not someone a woman who had just lost the man of her dreams and had been married to for thirty years would consider rebounding to.

Avery climbed in the Bronco and started the engine. He backed around and headed up the road, hoping for a call over his radio, anything to take his mind off of Josie.

5

Cole felt a heavy compression on his back. A massive efflux of water gushed up through his throat and spewed out his mouth forcing him to inhale deeply with a wheezing gasp. He opened his left eye slowly as the right side of his face was pressed in the gravelly mud.

A hand gripped his shoulder, and when he turned over, he was gazing up at Kate.

"Jesus, Cole. What the hell? I thought you were dead." She scowled then leaned down and kissed him on the clean side of his face.

Cole sat up with Kate's help, surprised that he was even alive. "Thanks for saving me."

"What are you talking about?"

"For dragging me out of the water."

"You were on the bank when I found you."

"I was? But how?" Cole wondered aloud, thinking by some miracle he had dislodged his foot out from under the rock and had drifted downstream and somehow washed ashore. But none of that made any sense. He was certain he had drowned. He glanced across the creek and remembered seeing the meadow before the trees.

He was positive this was the same spot.

The only difference was the boulder. The big rock was closer to the shore, almost as if a crane had picked it up, swung it ten feet, and dumped it back in the water.

He turned and saw his bucket and gold pan on the bank.

How did they get there?

Cole drew Kate's attention to the boulder. "That's the same rock that had me trapped but somehow it moved."

"I doubt that."

"It is, I swear."

"That rock has to weigh five hundred pounds. What, it just rolled over there all by itself?"

"I don't know."

A dark curtain came down through the trees, and with it, a slight breeze. Cole shivered as the sun began to dip behind the mountain ridge.

"We've got to get you out of these wet clothes," Kate said. "Boots first." She grabbed the heel of Cole's right rubber boot and pulled with all her might. It was difficult at first as his sock was soaked and had swollen inside the boot, but she managed to finally yank it off along with the sodden sock and did the same with his other boot.

"Okay, stand up," Kate said, grabbing him by the arm.

Kate helped Cole unsnap his wet shirt as his fingers were numb and pulled his arms out of the sleeves. Together they lifted his clinging T-shirt up over his head. Kate unbuckled Cole's belt and unzipped his jeans.

"Ga...ga...go girl," Cole stuttered, teeth chattering.

"Shut up, you dork."

Cole held on to her shoulder to balance as she tugged down each leg of his pants so he could step out.

"Panties too big boy."

"Don't....laugh." Cole grabbed his waistband and drew his damp underwear down around his ankles and kicked them off. He stood naked, shivering, and wrapped his arms around his chest.

Kate removed her flannel shirt. "Here, use this and dry yourself off." She happened a glance at his crotch. "Then you might want to cover Mister Nubby."

Once Cole had toweled off, he handed back her shirt. Kate took it and gathered Cole's clothes and boots and they headed back to the camp.

Cole could feel every pebble poking into the soles of his feet. It reminded him of the television commercial he'd always see illustrating diabetic nerve pain.

He was cold right down to his core and couldn't stop shaking.

Kate ran ahead and ducked into the tent. By the time he stepped into the campsite, Kate had retrieved a heavy sweatshirt, a pair of jeans, and his hiking boots with thick socks tucked inside and placed them on the log. Trembling, Cole got into his clothes. He sat on the log, slipped on the socks and boots, and stood, stomping the ground to get warm.

When he'd gotten the feeling back in his hands, Cole gathered some sticks and formed a teepee over a handful of dry moss in the fire pit. He lit the tinder and blew on the small flame until it rose up into the upright twigs and the fire caught enough for him to add small branches. Soon he had a rip-roaring fire going.

Cole crouched in front of the fire, and before he realized, it was nightfall.

Kate went back to the tent and came back with Cole's down ski jacket. She'd slipped on her hooded parka as the temperature had dropped ten degrees since the sun had gone down.

They huddled together on the log.

Cole looked up at the night sky. Stars were beginning to appear like bright gem stones drifting up from a tar pit. His hand touched something on the log. It was Kate's MP3 player. Out of curiosity, he picked it up and searched for the last song Kate had been listening to before she went looking for him.

It was *Love Shack* by the B-52's.

"Looking for something?" Kate asked.

"No, just a crazy thought that was running through my head while I was drowning," Cole said matter-of-factly, like his frightening ordeal was now no big deal.

"Yeah, and what was that?"

"You'd be listening to this song when you found my body and would never get it out of your head."

Kate leaned over to see the screen on her media player. "That wasn't it."

"Thank God. Imagine that stuck in your head. What were you listening to?"

"*Umbrella* by Rihanna."

6

Marcus had set up a lantern in the field so he could see in the dark. He pushed the filled wheelbarrow over toward the two separate piles that he had created throughout the afternoon and early evening.

One was a burn pile, which was made up of unwanted furniture they had dragged out of the farmhouse, and old, rotted wood from the fences he had torn down and scraps he had collected around the property.

The other heap was mostly metal or things too toxic for a bonfire. He'd haul it all away in his truck later to the nearest dumpsite.

He was pleased with their progress. As soon as Libby had resigned herself to the monumental task ahead of them, she tackled it head on, starting with clearing out much of Marcus' grandfather's things that they had no use for. Some of which were stored in the barn.

Knowing that Kaylee would soon become bored cleaning the farmhouse, Libby made a game of it, and soon their daughter was running around with a broom, sweeping here and there, pretending she was the Emma Watson character Hermione Granger from the Harry Potter series. When she lost interest in that, Libby set Kaylee up at the kitchen table with some color pencils and a sketchpad while Libby cleared out the cabinets and got rid of spoiled and expired food containers.

When Libby opened the refrigerator and gasped, "Oh my God!" and stepped back, Marcus thought for sure a rat had crawled inside and died, but it was just more rancid food. It stunk so bad they had to bag up everything and take it outside. After Marcus removed the racks, Libby gave the fridge a thorough cleaning with a thick sponge and a bucket of hot water and Pine-Sol cleaner.

They'd brought along their own foodstuff in grocery bags and ice coolers so they could restock some of the shelves and replace the perishables in the refrigerator once it had aired out enough and the smell was gone so they wouldn't have to make a run to the nearest supermarket which was a considerable distance away. Living way out in the country meant stocking up and less frequent trips to the store.

Marcus raised the handles and dumped the load of decayed wooden posts out of the wheelbarrow onto the burn pile. That was enough for one day. He picked up the lantern, placed it in the wheelbarrow, and headed toward the barn.

Once inside, he placed the lantern on the workbench and parked the wheelbarrow up against the wall. He thought tomorrow he might do some painting and decided to see what he could use that was on the shelves. He grabbed a paint can by the handle and picked it up. He could tell by its weight the can was about empty. He wondered how many other cans were on the shelves that should have been thrown out.

He figured it wouldn't hurt to take a few minutes and check each can.

Each time he found a can that he knew he couldn't use, he placed it on the ground. The ones that showed some promise, he put back on the shelf. Soon, there was a short stack of twenty or more paint cans on the dirt that he would later take out to the pile of junk designated for the dumps.

He'd lucked out and found four one-gallon paint cans that were still full and hadn't been opened; and according to the outside labels were for the interior and the same color—beige. He lined the cans up next to the lantern.

After digging around a cardboard box on the bottom shelf, he found some decent paintbrushes, a pan, and some rollers. Everything he needed to transform the walls of the dreary farmhouse into a cheery home. That would be tomorrow's project. He knew once he was done it would give Libby a brighter perspective on their new home.

He put the cardboard box on the workbench and was about to grab the lantern when he heard a sound in the back of the barn.

His first instinct was he might have to defend himself so he grabbed the pitchfork leaning up against the wall. With the lantern in one hand and the pitchfork pointed in front of him in his other hand, Marcus stepped slowly toward the rear of the building.

"I can hear you back there!" he yelled, hoping to scare whatever it was away.

Instead of scampering feet, Marcus heard a deep, rumbling gruff; almost on the verge of a growl. The menacing sound lasted for a good five seconds. He couldn't tell if it was a vicious warning or if the thing was just annoyed by his presence. Like he was the intruder instead of the other way around.

"You better get the hell out of here!" Growing up as a kid in a rough neighborhood, Marcus knew he had to be tougher than the other kids if he didn't want to get beat up. Which meant never backing down. If he didn't do it then, why should he start now.

"I'm warning you!" he shouted.

He stomped around the partition.

The light shone in his eyes as he held up the kerosene lantern, illuminating the rear stall. Marcus was ready to jab the pitchfork's tines at anything that came at him, but nothing did. The only thing in the stall was the same heap of straw.

The rear door was open. He couldn't remember whether he had closed it properly or left it ajar.

He heard a howl outside but it wasn't an animal.

It was the wind. Playing tricks. He sighed with relief having dreaded the thought of an encounter with a dangerous animal, and even if he had scared it off, he'd have to constantly worry about his family's safety.

Marcus got right to work and spent the next fifteen minutes boarding up the rear door.

7

Lou Cobb rolled over in bed and gave Arlene's shoulder a firm nudge with his stubby finger. His wife snorted and rolled over on her side. She always complained it was Lou's snoring that kept her up at night, but he knew she was the real culprit. There were times in the night when she would snap at him to "Shut the hell up!"

"How can I be snoring when I'm not even asleep?" was his usual retort.

Most nights he would toss and turn. He'd constantly be fluffing his pillow and could never seem to get comfortable. Maybe it was time for a new mattress or a bigger bed. Sleeping next to Arlene in their twin bed was like trying to fit both feet in one sock. He'd always have an arm or a leg draped over the edge. It was a miracle he hadn't fallen out of bed and cracked his skull wide open. Then maybe Arlene would stop harping on at him.

Arlene had been nagging him to get one of those CPAP machines. Sleep apnea or not, Lou knew there was no way he was going to get any rest wearing a dumb mask and having to listen to some pump all night. She should be the one wearing it, not him.

The mattress sagged as he turned over on his back and stared up at the ceiling. It was hopeless. Arlene started in again, this time louder than before, like a damn foghorn.

"Jesus, almighty!" he swore and rolled out of bed. It had been cold at bedtime so he'd slept in his long johns and a pair of thick, woolen socks. Arlene was always saying she couldn't understand how he could be cold with all his insulation, not that she had any room to talk.

Lou went over to the window and looked out. A crescent moon just over the treetops cast a dim, silvery glow over the sheep pens.

Lately, he'd had to separate some of his ewes as they had come down with chlamydia, and as a result, some stillbirths. The lambs that did survive had been frail and needed Arlene's special attention and nurturing. After docking a lamb's tail to prevent fly strike—a condition where maggots would burrow into the skin—the youngling died as it had been so weak before the elastrator could cut off the circulation for the tail to drop off. Lou hoped to resolve the problem of enzootic abortions by keeping the infected ewes separated from the rest of the flock and treating them with tetracycline.

During the night, the Cobbs kept their one hundred sheep congregated in four animal pens to protect them from nocturnal predators. At daybreak, Lou would usher the healthy sheep out of their pens and shepherd the large flock over to the hilly pastureland to graze behind their house while Arlene tended to the sick animals.

As an added precaution Lou had set up six sodium-vapor floodlights along the edge of the forest by the stockades. Each light was mounted high on a tree trunk and was activated by a motion detector and would remain lit for twenty seconds then go off after the sensor had been triggered if there was no longer any movement. The sudden bright light was enough to scare off any intruder.

He turned away from the window and glanced over at the bed. Arlene had stopped snoring. Maybe now, he could get back in bed and get some much-needed sleep. He shuffled across the hardwood floor in his stocking feet and was about to sit on the edge of the mattress when a thin beam of light shone into the room.

Lou jumped up and rushed to the window.

The floodlight farthest from the house had come on.

He gazed at the sheep, huddled together in their pens. They were agitated, bleating and stamping their hooves. One of the rams was butting a side railing to escape, sensing danger from the nearby woods.

Lou backed away from the window. "Arlene! Wake up!"

She groggily opened her eyes. "What..."

"Something's scaring the sheep."

Arlene must have heard the restless sheep because she immediately sat up in bed. "What is it?"

"I don't know," Lou said and charged out of the bedroom. He knew Arlene would be right behind as he hurried down the stairs. He stomped through the kitchen into the mudroom. He sat on the bench and pulled on his Wellington rubber boots. Arlene had thrown on her dressing gown from the bedroom and was coming in just as Lou stood and grabbed his flannel-lined coat from a hook on the wall.

Arlene plopped down on the bench to put on her boots.

Lou unlocked the footlocker by the door. He took out a twin-barrel shotgun, opened the breech to make sure there were fresh cartridges inside, and snapped the barrel shut. He took some extra shells and stuffed them in the side pocket of his coat.

Arlene grabbed a flashlight. "I'm ready, let's go."

Lou pushed through the screen door and stepped outside.

They strode across the yard keeping far enough away from the edge of the forest so as not to trigger the other security lights.

The far floodlight went dark as they passed the first enclosure.

"What do you think?" Arlene whispered as they both stopped.

"Quiet." Lou raised the barrel of the shotgun and pointed the muzzle at the trees.

The sheep behind them seemed less distressed and were no longer as tense as before and were settling down as if Lou and Arlene's presence was enough to calm the jittery animals.

Lou stared into the trees but it was too dark to see anything but rough-edge silhouettes. He cocked his head and listened for a moment. The wind had picked up, disguising any sounds that may be out there.

"Oh my," Arlene said.

Lou turned to his wife. "What?"

"Look." Arlene held her hand out and a tiny snowflake landed on her palm.

They looked up and saw the night sky dotted with accumulating specks of white snow.

"We better get back inside," Lou said.

"What about the sheep?"

"Whatever was out there, I'm sure it's gone."

The flurry graduated into heavier snowfall as they started back to the house, their boots crunching over the frozen ground.

Lou knew he didn't have to worry about the sheep as most of them were overdue for shearing and had thick coats that would protect them from the bitter cold.

His main concern at the moment was returning to bed and hopefully getting back to sleep before Arlene started up again warning ships to stay away from the rocks.

8

Marcus heard a scream and jumped out of bed. Wearing only a T-shirt and a pair of briefs, he dashed barefoot out of the bedroom to Kaylee's room.

The door was open, but Kaylee wasn't in her bed.

Libby had gotten up and was standing in the doorway. "What's going on?"

"Kaylee's gone."

"Oh my God."

Marcus spun around in a panic, searching the room.

"You don't think..." but Libby stopped before finishing when Marcus exchanged the dreaded look that they were sharing the same paranoid thought that always came to mind when they were living in the city. That someone had abducted their daughter.

Kaylee's window was closed, which meant that whoever had taken their daughter had found another way to sneak into the house.

He turned, sprang for the front door.

It was already open so he ran outside...

And saw Kaylee outside, playing in the snow.

"Kaylee!" Marcus yelled, more relieved than angry.

His daughter looked up and squealed with joy. "Hi, Daddy! Come play with me!"

"Oh my, Marcus. We must have slept right through the storm," Libby said.

There was more than two inches of snow on the ground and the surrounding forest looked like a giant lot of flocked Christmas trees. The barn's slanted roof was white. The heap of junk and the burn pile looked like confectionary on top a field of vanilla ice cream.

Marcus was glad to see that his daughter had the sense to put on a coat and gloves before coming outside as he stood in his underwear, shivering. "Hold on, Kaylee. Let me throw on some clothes."

"I'll go put on a pot of coffee," Libby said as they rushed back to their bedroom to get dressed.

A minute later, Marcus was stomping down the snow-covered porch steps while Libby went into the kitchen.

"Let me grab a shovel," Marcus said, heading toward the barn. "And we can build a snowman."

Even though Kaylee was wearing gloves, Marcus could tell they were already soaked through, as they weren't water-repellent. If he had known it was going to snow so early in the season, he would have made sure they were properly prepared. Either way, it was exciting for Kaylee as this was the first time she had ever been in the snow.

Marcus trudged through the ankle-deep snow and opened the barn door.

He went inside, found a wide-blade snow shovel leaning up against the wall, and carried it outside. It made the job so much easier and it wasn't long before Marcus had scooped enough snow in a pile so they could start building the lower section of the snowman. Once they'd rounded the compacted snow, Marcus and Kaylee worked on the next stage for the upper torso. Marcus lifted the white sphere and placed it on top of the base.

Kaylee found two sticks—one twice as long as the other—and stuck each one on as twig arms.

Libby came outside, carrying two steaming cups of coffee. She stood next to Marcus and handed him his mug. "So, how's it coming along?" she asked and took a sip of her coffee.

"Still a work in progress," Marcus said, taking a drink of his coffee and placing the mug on the ground. He got down on his knees and began rolling some snow for the head while Kaylee ran off to collect some small rocks for the face.

Marcus molded the snow into the shape of a soccer ball and placed it on top of the other two spheres. Kaylee came back and handed Marcus the stones. He added the eyes and formed a happy face grin with the pebbles.

"What should we use for the nose, Daddy?"

"Well, normally a carrot." Marcus turned to Libby but she shook her head.

"I'll go inside and see what I can find," Libby said. She walked back, taking sips of her coffee as she went up the porch steps and into the house.

Marcus retrieved his mug from the ground. It was still warm despite being left in the snow. He took a gulp and looked at Kaylee. She was shivering, standing with her arms down at her sides, as her gloves were wet. Each time she exhaled, a misty vapor would puff out of her mouth. Her nose and cheeks were ruddy from the cold.

"Want to go inside, warm up?" Marcus asked.

"No way, Daddy." She looked up and gave him a big smile.

Libby came out and hurried down the steps. She had left her coffee cup behind. She was carrying something in her hand.

"I hope this will suffice," Libby said and handed Marcus a large pickle.

He took the kosher dill, looked at it for a moment then inserted the brined cucumber under the snowman's eyes for the finishing touch.

The Pike family admired their very first snowman.

"Well, what do you think, Kaylee?" Marcus said. "Should we give him a name?"

Kaylee pondered the question then blurted out, "I know. Let's call him Booger Face because he has a green nose."

"Kaylee!" Libby couldn't believe what just came out of their daughter's mouth.

"Then Booger Face it is," Marcus grinned and they all started laughing.

9

Cole unzipped the tent and crawled out first. "Kate, this is incredible."

Kate followed him out on her hands and knees. They stood together, gazing out at the wintry landscape. A thick blanket of snow covered the terrain. The rocks and boulders in the stream were crowned with white-capped domes; the trees white pyramids stretching up into the mist-shrouded mountain.

"We should take a selfie for our next Christmas card," Kate said. She reached into her parka and took out her smartphone. She held the device out at arm's length and moved closer to Cole. "Say limburger."

Cole and Kate smiled for the camera and said, "Cheese," as Kate snapped a couple of pictures. She looked at the screen, smiled approvingly, and swiped to the next image.

"Maybe it would be better if we posed with our gold pans," Cole said. "Showed off a little."

"You really want our friends to know what we really do out here?"

"Yeah, maybe you're right." As much as Cole liked to brag about prospecting like the old-timers back in the days of the Gold Rush, he knew Kate was right. Better to keep it on the lowdown. He certainly didn't want their friends encroaching on their good fortune.

Nothing dissolved a friendship faster than money. First mention of their gold claim, every so-called friend they had would insistently impose themselves wanting a piece of the action.

Which was why none of their friends knew where they were. Maybe not the best strategy, hiking out into the wilderness without giving anyone a head's up, but then Cole and Kate had always been spontaneous and adventurous, even before they were married.

"I'll boil some water for coffee," Cole said. He went over to the log. He'd covered the camping equipment with a tarp to keep everything dry in the event it should rain, having no inclination it was going to snow during the night.

He set up the portable camp stove, opening the valve on the small propane tank, and pushed the starter button. He adjusted the valve to control the flame.

Kate went over to the stream and filled a pot with water. She came back, handed the metal container to Cole, and he set it on the burner.

Digging in her backpack, Kate came up with two packets of Folgers instant coffee. She placed them next to their aluminum mugs.

Once the water had boiled, Cole filled their cups with hot water while Kate added the freeze-dried granules and stirred.

Cole looked around, amazed at how beautiful everything looked: the ambling creek, the snow-covered trees, and the tulle fog on the mountain. It didn't get any better than this. He gripped his mug by the handle.

"Hmm," Cole said, his nose over his cup, taking a whiff of the steaming brew. "Nothing beats..."

A loud, jarring noise sounded upriver.

Cole lowered his cup. "What the hell?"

"What is that?" Kate asked.

"Sounds like an outboard."

"What, a boat?"

"We better go see." Of all the times they'd worked their claim, Cole and Kate had never seen another soul and always had the picturesque spot all to themselves. It wasn't like they were indifferent to hikers happening by, they just preferred the private seclusion. Cole wondered if maybe a group had floated down in a river raft or one of those flat-bottom boats, which was unlikely this time of year.

This certainly wasn't how he wanted to start his day. Being questioned by a bunch of strangers if they should come ashore. Convincing them they were trespassing even though they truly weren't, just a ruse to get them to clear out and keep on going.

They left their coffee mugs on the log and walked along the bank toward the ruckus. Cole figured whatever it was making all the racket had to be a quarter mile away, round a bend farther up.

He had his GPS-enabled PDA along with a printed map showing the boundaries of their gold claim in his jacket pocket as proof if anyone should challenge him. It had been a while since Cole and Kate had ventured up to the northern most region of their claim site as they'd been having marginal success where they were currently camped.

When they came to a bend, Cole and Kate took their time crossing over the slippery snow-covered rocks. The snow had a tendency to clump between the boulders giving the impression it was solid. One false step and they'd fall through and break an ankle.

The source of the sound was just up ahead.

Cole and Kate crouched and crept up to a bush. They peered through the branches.

A burly man wearing a dirty thermal shirt with the sleeves rolled up and hip waders was standing in the stream next to a dredge pump floating on twin pontoons. He held a large hose with both hands and was siphoning the bottom with a nozzle. The loud gasoline engine on the rig was driving the pump that was sucking up debris and discharging it into a sluice box.

Two other men with scruffy beards and wearing grubby overalls were working a quarry, digging up a muddy embankment with shovels, and feeding the material into a large rotating cylinder driven by another generator. They had broad chests with bulging biceps and looked like they could be related. It was easy to imagine them as a tag-team in the World Wrestling Federation.

"Son of a bitch!" Cole started to stand but Kate pulled him back down.

"What are you doing?"

"I'm going to tell them to get the hell off our claim," Cole said, looking at Kate who was still staring through the shrub.

"That might not be a good idea."

Cole turned and peered through the bushes.

A fourth man had appeared from behind the trees. He had a bushy red beard and looked older than the others, possessing an air of authority suggesting that he was in charge. He was also cradling something in the crook of his arm.

Cole strained to get a better look. "Oh shit. Is that a shotgun?"

10

Josie Mills cut across the snow on her property and followed the path through the trees. It was a shortcut Lewis had blazed years ago leading over to Ray Pike's farm. The half-mile trail was flat and made for a pleasant stroll through the forest.

Duke, her chocolate lab, bounded ahead sniffing and exploring the unexpected winter wonderland. Six years old and weighing a whopping 100 pounds, Duke was a big dog with unlimited energy.

Josie reached a fallen juniper straddling the creek that served as an adequate footbridge. Lewis had used a chainsaw to trim the branches at the proper height so as to serve as posts and stretched lengths of rope for handrails on either side of the trunk, which was wide enough to cross without too much difficulty even with the thin crust of ice.

Duke chose to wade through the chilly, shallow stream as Josie stepped warily across the crude footbridge. The path continued on the other side for another hundred yards onto the Pike parcel.

Josie saw a truck she didn't recognize parked next to the farmhouse. Duke raced across the yard and stopped a few feet short of a funny-looking snowman. It looked like a partial amputee and had a green nose of all things.

Duke let out a loud bark.

Josie expected Duke to charge the snowman. Instead, the dog raised a hind leg and let loose a steady stream of warm pee creating a steamy yellow hole.

The front door opened and a young man stepped out onto the porch. He had paint splatter on his clothes and was holding a brush. As soon as he saw Josie, he put his brush on the porch railing, and rushed down the steps.

"Josie! How have you been?"

"Marcus, is that you?"

"Sure is." Marcus gave Josie a welcoming hug. He glanced back at the front door. "Libby! Kaylee! Come see who's here."

Josie saw an attractive young woman and a little girl come out of the house.

"This is Josie. Josie and her husband were good friends of my grandfather." As soon as he said that, he gave Josie an apologetic look. "I was so sorry to hear about Lewis."

"Thank you. I miss them both dearly."

Marcus took a moment to introduce Libby and Kaylee, as they had never met Josie before. They talked for a few minutes, getting further acquainted.

Kaylee saw Duke sitting next to the snowman and saw what he had done.

"Bad dog!" Kaylee ran toward the big dog.

"Marcus?" Libby said, fearing for their daughter's safety.

"It's okay," Josie said. "He's going to think it's a game. You just watch."

Before Kaylee could get close enough to scold the offending dog, Duke was on his feet, jumping around, and ready to play. It was so comical to watch that Kaylee couldn't help but laugh. Duke thought it would be fun to run around the snowman and quickly got Kaylee to join in.

"See, I told you," Josie said. "He's just one big doofus."

"So, do you live far?" Libby asked.

"No, just over the creek and through those trees," Josie said, nodding over her shoulder. She glanced around and saw the two large piles of debris in the snow. "I see you've been busy."

"I'm working on a burn pile," Marcus said.

"Make sure to get a burn permit."

"Where do I get one?"

"Our local fire marshal."

Marcus noticed Josie giving the chicken coop a critical appraisal with its mishmash of different building materials. "I guess my grandfather wasn't much of a carpenter."

"Oh, there was a time Ray kept the place up, but after your grandmother passed, well, you know."

"Would you like to come in and see what we've done?"

"Yes, I would." Josie looked across the yard. Duke and Kaylee were standing near the edge of the woods. Something had their attention.

Marcus called out, "Kaylee, we're going into the house!"

Kaylee turned and ran across the yard.

Duke remained. His head was down, shoulders hunched, hackles straight up like black porcupine spines. The rumbling in his chest was so loud it could be heard all the way to the porch.

"What's he doing? Is he growling?" Marcus said as they went onto the porch.

"Duke, get over here now!" Josie called out.

The big dog didn't respond.

"Come, boy!"

Duke turned and sprinted after Kaylee.

"What was Duke growling at?" Marcus asked Kaylee as she came scampering up the porch steps.

"I *don't* know. I didn't see anything," she replied, dashing into the house.

"That was weird," Marcus said to Josie.

"Probably nothing," Josie replied, taking a quick glance at the woods before going inside.

11

Cole never thought for a minute they'd be dealing with claim jumpers, especially one armed with a pistol-grip shotgun. Before he'd married Kate, Cole enjoyed hanging out at the local gym where he'd picked up some basics boxing and learned a few self-defense tactics. It was more of an excuse to hang out with his buddies than anything else so he never took it seriously. Not even when a close friend with a black belt in karate tried to get him to enroll in his class.

Now he wished he'd taken his friend up on the invite. Not that he'd consider jumping out and going kung fu on these guys. That would be suicide. These four were serious trouble.

"We have to get out of here," Kate said, keeping her voice low even though there was no way the men could hear her over the two loud generators.

Cole put his hand up. "Not yet."

The man out in the stream reached over and shut off his generator. "I need a break," he said and trudged through the water. He paused and grabbed a six-pack of beer that had been chilling in the frigid stream.

The two working the tumbler threw down their shovels and one of them shut off the other generator. They ambled over to the man coming out of the water. He pulled a couple cans from the plastic ring and tossed each man a beer. The three opened the tabs with metallic *snaps* and foam spurted out. They guzzled the beer and crumpled the aluminum in their beefy hands, throwing the empty cans on the ground.

Cole spotted a can in the mud that hadn't been crushed—Olympia—just like the smashed cans they'd found at their campsite. So, it was these jerks that had pulled out their sign and thrown it in the bushes. The nerve.

The man with the red beard put out his hand. "Gimme one."

"Sure thing, Red." The man in the waders pulled off a can.

Red leaned the shotgun against a boulder and popped the tab on his beer. He put the can up to his mouth and took a gulp. Froth dripped off his beard.

One of the men that had been shoveling dirt into the tumbler walked over and looked inside the large cylinder. He reached in and shifted through the material with his hand. "Hey, will you look at this?" He turned, looked at Red, and held up a gold nugget—the size of a soap dish.

"Damn, Seth. I told you boys this was the place," Red said and took another swallow of his beer.

"Yeah? I haven't found diddlysquat out there in the creek," griped the man in the waders.

"That's cause you ain't lucky like Jesse and me," Seth boasted.

"Oh, yeah. I'll show you who's lucky..."

"Back down, Boyd," Red said in a stern voice. "No need getting all riled. Everyone gets an even split."

"What, that ain't fair. Jesse and I do all the work breaking our backs and we're expected to hand over a share to Boyd."

"That's right, dipshit," Boyd grinned.

"The hell," Jesse said. "Seth's right. Boyd don't deserve that."

"You boys arguing with me?"

Seth and Jesse looked at each other then Seth turned to Red. "No, sir."

"Then it's settled. Seth, bring that bucket over here."

Seth stepped around the tumbler and grabbed a pail. He carried it over to a metal pan, grabbed the lip and the bottom, and dumped out half a bucket of gold nuggets—

At least twenty pounds

—Worth somewhere in the neighborhood of $400,000.

"We're rich boys," Red said.

"They hell you are!" Cole blurted out.

The four men turned as Cole stood up and stepped out from behind the bushes.

"Jesus, Cole. What are you doing?" Kate pleaded, trying to stop him but he was too mad to listen to reason.

"Who the hell are you?" Red said, glaring at Cole.

"You're trespassing."

"What, you own this mountain?"

"No, but this is our claim."

"Your claim?"

"That's right. And I have proof," Cole said, digging in his pocket. He took out the printed map and held it out. "Take a look for yourself."

Red looked at his men then walked up to Cole, who was relieved that the man hadn't picked up the shotgun. Maybe there was a chance to reason with them.

The old man snatched the map from Cole's hand. He looked at the map, turned it over even though the other side was blank, and went tsk-tsk then ripped it up.

"What are you doing?" Cole asked, not believing the old man had actually done that.

"Last time I checked, this was a free country," Red said, shaking his head and tossing the pieces of paper up in the air.

"I could have you arrested."

"I doubt that."

Kate grabbed Cole by the arm. "Come on, Cole. We need to go."

"Maybe you should listen to your girlfriend."

"She's not my girlfriend, she's my wife."

"Is that so?" Red said. He glanced over at Seth and Jesse. Both men had big grins on their faces. Boyd had been standing with his arms crossed behind the old man.

Cole looked at the gold nuggets in the pan. "This is our claim, so rightfully, that belongs to us."

"Oh yeah, good luck proving it," Red said, directing Cole's attention to the torn strips strewn on the ground.

"I can, right here." Cole reached in his coat and pulled out his PDA-GPS.

Boyd stepped around Red, snatched the device out of Cole's hand, and threw it in the creek. "Not anymore."

"Cole! Let's go!" Kate was trying to pull him away.

Maybe she was right. This was getting them nowhere. Best not to cause trouble. He could file a grievance with the county recorder; maybe get the local sheriff involved.

"Okay, have it your way. You'll be hearing from us."

"I don't think so," Red said.

Cole turned. He'd been too distracted arguing with Red that he hadn't noticed Seth sneaking up behind him with a shovel.

Kate screamed as Seth swung the blade at Cole's head.

And then everything went black.

12

Lou got his equipment ready in the shearing shed as the ten sheep bleated in the small corral. He laid out a ground cloth for catching the wool so it wouldn't get further soiled on the dirt floor under the hanging sling that he used to drape over to support his back. Bending over a hundred-pound sheep and getting it positioned so he could run the clippers was backbreaking work.

"I'm ready for the first one," Lou said.

Arlene opened the gate to the stall and shooed out a thick-fleeced ram. She shut the gate and the animal followed her calmly over to where Lou was standing as it knew the routine.

Lou leaned over the sling and turned the ram so that it was standing facing away from him. He grabbed the sheep under the chest and tipped it onto its rump so that all four legs were off the ground.

Arlene gave Lou a hand shear with a powered-driven toothed blade that was attached to a long flexible shaft that contained the cord and extended up to an electric motor mounted on a tall stand.

"You can turn it on." As soon as Arlene switched on the motor, Lou began running the clippers under the ram's thick coat. Lou made a clean pass down to the bare skin. He lifted up the section of wool then sheared some more, doing his best to keep the fleece in one piece if possible. That way, it would be easier for Arlene to wash and hang to dry.

With the arrival of the early snow, it was important to keep the sheep indoors that Lou was planning to shear today, as they wouldn't have the wool to protect them from the cold. He was shearing these particular sheep because their coats had gotten too thick and he was worried they might suffer in the dreary weather. Wool fibers were hollow and hydroscopic so they held moisture and weighed the animals down.

Lou made sure he didn't harm the ram as he repositioned it so he could get at the different parts of its body. He loved his animals and always treated them with respect, even the cantankerous ones.

Arlene often kidded him that he treated the sheep better than he treated her.

Being an old pro he was done with the animal in just under two minutes, as he wasn't in any particular hurry. Arlene switched off the shearing motor.

The ram was glad to be back on its feet and did a little dance.

"Aren't you the frisky one," Arlene said with a laugh and led the bald sheep back to the enclosure.

She came back with a sheep that looked like a giant cotton ball with sticks for legs. "I like the natural crimp on this one."

"Nice fleece for hand spinning," Lou said, noting the thin wool on the animal.

Through the years, Lou and Arlene had established good working relationships with both local and out-of-state weavers and spinners who were interested in the Cobb's high-quality wool.

Arlene led the sheep over...

An ungodly howl sounded outside.

Lou turned and stared at the closed door that led out to the pens.

"Lou, *what* was that?" Arlene asked.

"I don't rightly know."

The sheep inside the stockade crowded together nervously.

Lou could hear the sheep bleating outside, their hooves stampeding over the ground, bodies banging against the fence railings.

"Something's attacking the sheep." He ran for the door.

"Lou, don't go out there."

He stopped and looked back at Arlene. "I have to. Damn, I wish I had my gun."

A sheep outside cried in agony.

Lou glanced around for a weapon and saw a pitchfork next to a bale of hay that they used to feed the animals residing in the shed. He grabbed the tool and started for the door.

"You can't go out there with that."

"It's better than nothing." Lou had no idea what he would be facing but it was better than going out there barehanded. He wanted nothing better than to kill the miserable thing, but hoped it had run off and not injured the other sheep. He looked forward to hunting it down. It wouldn't be hard to track in the snow.

He reached out, unlatched the door, and kicked it open.

The first thing he saw was all the blood. It looked especially red in the snow. "Son of a bitch!" He stomped out with the pitchfork.

The end of a top railing had been yanked from the post and was lying diagonally on the ground.

One of the Cobb's best wool producers—a one hundred-fifty pound ewe—was lying on its side in a crimson ring. The animal was close to death. Its tongue hung out, vapor still escaping its mouth. The sheep's belly had been sliced wide open; steamy entrails unfurled in the red snow.

It pained Lou to see the animal suffer, so it was almost a relief when the ewe took its last panting breath.

"Lou, look!" Arlene said, pointing.

Lou saw churned up ground and a blood trail leading into the trees. The predator must have dragged off one of the sheep, muddling the tracks.

He turned and started for the house.

Arlene ran after him.

"Don't go alone," she pleaded.

"I need to get out there. Catch it when it stops to eat."

"Wait!" Arlene grabbed Lou's arm and turned him around. "Have you already forgotten what happened to Lewis and Ray?"

Lou looked at Arlene but didn't say anything.

"We need to phone Avery. It won't take him long to get here."

Lou realized how frightened Arlene was for his safety. If anything should happen to him, she would be on her own. He knew she would struggle without him and it would be an overbearing hardship running the farm all alone.

His death would send her to an early grave.

"All right," Lou agreed. "We'll call him."

13

Avery drove up in his Ford Bronco and parked in a turnaround next to the Cobb's home. He grabbed his Stetson off the passenger seat and climbed out of the vehicle. He squared his hat on his head, zipped up his foul-weather jacket to ward off the cold.

"Over here!" hollered Lou Cobb, standing by the sheep pens beside his wife, Arlene.

The sheriff stepped across the hard-packed snow. "I hear you had some trouble?"

"See for yourself," Lou answered.

Avery walked up to the couple and stared down at the mutilated sheep. "Any idea what it was?"

"I don't think it was coyotes, they usually only come out at night."

"Wolves?"

"We heard it howl. But it didn't sound like any wolf I've ever heard," Arlene said.

"How long has it been?"

"Close to an hour," Lou replied. "I'm ready to set out if you are?" He had his 12-gauge with the breech open, cartridges stuffed in the twin tubes.

"I'll go grab my carbine." Avery walked back to the Bronco. He stuck his key into the rear door and lowered the back window. He reached inside, grabbed his Winchester lever-action. He took out a box of ammo and stuffed it in the side pocket of his coat.

When he came back Lou was waiting for him at the edge of the forest. Arlene had retrieved a hammer from the shed and was nailing the fallen railing back to the post.

Avery and Lou went into the woods.

They followed the blood trail through the trees and up a slight slope. There were spots where the snow had melted, leaving slushy patches of mud.

After ten more minutes of hiking, Avery commented, "Pretty unusual for a predator to drag its prey this far, wouldn't you say?"

"Must be damn strong. None of my sheep weigh under a hundred pounds."

They were coming up on some boulders, which made the going tougher. A slick swath of blood stained the rocks.

Avery scaled the first rock then climbed up on a stone ledge gouged into the base of a snowy hillock, and that is when he discovered the sheep's carcass.

The hide had been stripped off in parts, huge bite marks with large sections of flesh eaten away. Its stomach cavity and ribcage were hollowed out, the internal organs gone. If Avery hadn't known what they were searching for, he would never have guessed what kind of animal the mutilated remains had been.

Lou joined him on the flat rock and stared at what was left of his sheep. "This looks more like the work of a mountain lion."

"That's a lot of mutton for one meal," Avery said. "They usually like to hide their kill and come back to feed. There's not much left here."

"Must have a big appetite, whatever it is."

Avery looked around the blood-splattered rock then up the snow-covered hillside. "That's odd. I don't see any tracks."

"Let's split up. There's got to be something."

"Don't go far. For all we know, this thing could be watching us right now."

Avery set out in one direction while Lou went the other way.

They hadn't been separated for more than a minute when Lou called out, "Over here!"

Avery turned and headed toward Lou's voice.

"What do you make of this?" Lou asked as Avery rushed over.

Both men stared at the giant footprint in a patch of snow between a jumble of rocks that stretched up the sloping terrain and could have been a landslide at one time.

Lou stood one boot in the giant impression making sure his heel was touching the curved back edge. There was at least two inches on either side of his boot and six inches of space to the round indentations at the front of the footprint made by the bottoms of five very large toes.

"I wear a size-12 shoe," Lou said.

"Jesus," Avery said. "Could it be?"

"I'd say that's a Bigfoot."

14

Kate cried while Seth and Jesse dragged Cole off into the trees.

Boyd had tied her hands together in front and made her sit on a rock near the tumbler. He'd bound her feet and secured the rope around one of the metal legs so that she couldn't get away.

She couldn't get the image of Cole being walloped by the shovel out of her head. It had happened so fast. The blade had smacked him on the upper shoulder and the back of his head. As soon as he went down, she could see blood seeping out of his hair.

All the while, Red had stood by, not saying a word, like this kind of thing happened all the time and everyone knew their role without being told what do. He'd been so nonchalant about the whole thing, that he'd pulled a stubby cigar out of his shirt pocket and lit it up. Puffing away just as casually as can be.

For Red, it was business as usual: robbing and killing people.

Kate wanted to scream for help but knew it would be a waste of time; there was no one around to hear her and come to her rescue.

How foolish they had been, coming out here and not letting anyone know where they were. This was the kind of thing she'd seen in movies where the stupid young couple from the city with no survival skills goes off in the wilderness and is never heard from again. Killed by some wild animal or some backwoods clan. Or a bunch of greedy claim jumpers.

She couldn't stop worrying what they were going to do to her. When Boyd had tied her up, he hadn't said a word. No threats or leering taunts. It was like he was parking her out of the way so they could continue on with what they were doing. Maybe they hadn't planned to hurt her.

Yeah, right!

Wake up, Kate. The bastards just killed your husband.

Red blew out some smoke and ordered the other three men to get back to work.

Boyd waded back out into the stream. He fired up the generator on the pontoons, grabbed the big hose, and bent over to suck up the pebble bottom.

Seth cranked up the other generator and the tumbler started turning. Jesse grabbed a pail and shovel and walked off.

Seth dumped some material into the rotating cylinder, but had his eyes on Kate.

She knew exactly what was on his mind.

He looked over at Red, who had decided to go sit by the creek and watch Boyd work. Jesse had sauntered off with his pail and shovel looking for another spot to dig.

Seth made his move and pulled out his knife. He cut the rope and freed her feet then yanked her up and dragged her into the trees.

She knew even if she screamed the others couldn't hear her with the deafening generators and the rocks crashing inside the tumbler.

He waited until they were twenty feet back in the forest before he threw her down on the ground. He flicked the knife down and the blade stood up in the dirt. He straddled her waist, and unbuckled his belt.

Kate looked at the knife but it was just out of reach.

"Pull down those pants," he ordered.

"Go to hell," Kate shouted back. She caught a glimpse of a dark shadow lurking back in the trees.

"Then I'll do it for you, bitch." Seth lowered onto his knees. He grabbed the waistband of her jeans with both hands, and tugged...

A large cobblestone caved in the side of Seth's head destroying his left eye socket, cheek, and jawbone. His imploded skull looked like a half-deflated ball that had been pushed in. The sound reminded Kate of a Halloween when she accidentally dropped a pumpkin on the stoop steps and it went *Splat!*

The impact snapped his neck and his head flopped on his shoulder as he fell on top of her.

Kate was covered with pulverized bone chips and bits of brain and a face full of blood. She brought her hands up to wipe her eyes. She gave the nearly decapitated man a shove to one side to push him off.

Bright red blood shot out of his torn neck like a geyser as he fell over onto the ground.

Kate crawled over and grabbed the knife.

She sawed through the rope.

Something moved back behind the tree trunks. She didn't get a good look and then it was gone. She wanted to call out, thank whoever had thrown the rock but was afraid her voice would carry to where the men were working. Maybe it was someone that had a grudge with Seth and had hid in the woods waiting for the perfect opportunity to even a score.

Yeah, I'd say you evened the score, and some.

Kate scrambled to her feet. There wasn't time to lose; she had to get as far away from here as possible.

But not until she knew whether Cole was alive or not.

15

As sheriff, Avery had sworn an oath to uphold the law and protect the citizens, even the undesirable ones, which was why he was driving the steep treacherous road down to the river. He'd put the Bronco in four-wheel drive and downshifted into low gear so the all-terrain tires would have maximum traction in the mud and snow.

At one point he thought for sure he was going to slide off the hazardous lane that was really too narrow for a truck to pass and more suitable for motorcycles and ATV quads. Traffic meant for hoodlum bikers and backwoods locals looking to acquire a jug of illegal moonshine.

Avery drove to the end of the road and parked short of Kaine Brown's cabin. The slanted roof was covered with dried pine needles and blotches of snow. Both windows were covered with black material—most likely cut up trash bags—to keep curious eyes from peeking in. The place looked like a way station for derelicts.

He got out of the Bronco. He put on his hat, as it was official business and definitely not a social call.

As a precaution, he rested his right hand on the butt of his holstered Smith & Wesson .357 magnum revolver, and looked around.

Thirty feet from the cabin was an old equipment shed, the building slightly bigger than a two-car garage. Eight-foot wide twin doors were closed together in the front with a hasp for a padlock. Avery didn't see a lock on the doors.

He heard a whimper and turned.

It was a mangy mutt, a possible crossbreed between a coonhound and maybe an Alsatian chained to a spike in the ground. The thing was emaciated with a protruding ribcage and stomach sucked up between its hind legs. It looked like it hadn't eaten in weeks.

A weather-warped crate with missing slats served as a poor excuse for a doghouse in the snow. Nearby was a water dish with a top layer of frozen ice.

Avery was appalled. He walked over to the dog. It was slunk low on the snow with its tail between its scrawny legs.

"Hey there."

The dog cowered and retreated inside the crate.

"I'm not going to hurt you."

Two petrified eyes gazed out at the sheriff.

"Okay, then," Avery said and backed away, knowing he had to gain the dog's trust. He went back to the Bronco, reached through the open window, and grabbed the other half of his ham sandwich out of his lunch bag that he had been saving for later. He brought the food over and placed it on the ground a foot away from the entrance of the crate.

Giving the canine some space, Avery stepped back a few feet.

He looked down and saw the water dish. He drew his handgun, bent down, and broke up the ice with the butt of his weapon. He put his gun back in the holster then picked out the jagged pieces of ice. The water looked clean enough to drink so he picked up the bowl and carried it to the crate.

Avery was surprised to see the half sandwich gone, as he never heard the dog move from the crate, let alone eat. It must have gobbled it up in one bite and retreated back into the crate without him seeing.

"So what are you, the Flash?" Avery stood patiently for well over a minute, looking down at those pathetic eyes gazing back at him wondering how in the hell anyone could treat an animal so despicably.

He was starting to walk over to pull the stake out of the ground and free the dog when one of the doors on the equipment shed swung open.

Avery spun around.

Kaine Brown froze in the doorway. It was obvious by his startled expression that he hadn't been expecting anyone, especially the sheriff.

He was wearing a sidearm in a leather holster. Avery had seen him with the same gun: a Taurus 5-shot 38 special with a rubber handgrip. His hand slowly dropped, fingers brushing the leather.

"I'm here on a courtesy call," Avery said, figuring he better defuse the situation with some banter before they ended up in a ridiculous gunfight. There was no law that said people couldn't arm themselves on their own property, which made Avery's job extremely dangerous as it was difficult to distinguish a genuine threat from those just protecting themselves.

"Is that right?" Kaine reached back and made sure the door was closed behind him.

"There's something prowling the mountain. Killed some of Lou Cobb's sheep. Thought you should know."

"Oh, yeah? Sorry to hear that."

Avery knew he wasn't sorry and couldn't care less about his neighbors. Kaine was sounding sympathetic so Avery would leave. It was common knowledge that Kaine Brown kept a still in that equipment shed and was brewing moonshine and selling it cheap.

The drawback being law-abiding folks had to deal with the constant flow of unsavory types sneaking through the mountain and having to worry about the safety of their families and unwanted trespassers.

Attracting deviants like flies to manure.

But so far there hadn't been any trouble.

Avery figured if he shut the man's operation down, it would mean another moonshiner moving in to take his place and hiking up the price of hooch, which wouldn't set well with Kaine's regular customers.

And then there would be trouble.

Avery looked over at the crate for a second then turned to Kaine. "When was the last time you fed that dog?"

"Why, you want it? Take it. I don't want it."

"I have a better idea. How about I come pay you a visit, let's say, everyday, so I can check up on the dog? Make sure you're treating it good." Avery knew Kaine wouldn't like the idea of him coming around on a daily basis, as it would scare away his customers. Maybe give everyone the impression that Kaine and the sheriff had become buddies and were setting up a sting operation.

"Just take the damn dog," Kaine said.

"Maybe I will, but not today. See you around," Avery said, and tipped his hat. He walked toward the Bronco but kept one eye on Kaine as he did. Never smart to turn your back on a rattlesnake.

Avery climbed behind the wheel and started up the truck. He backed around and started back up the hill.

He looked over at the empty lunch bag on the passenger seat and thought of that poor dog shivering in that crate.

Kaine Brown, I'm going to make your life a living hell.

16

Kate knew she didn't have much time before her captors realized she was no longer tethered to the leg of the tumble barrel. Maybe Seth's absence wouldn't raise a red flag right away. The other men would probably assume he had taken her out into the woods to do whatever he pleased and their turn would come later. She doubted if these men had any morals as they did pretty much as they pleased; especially after witnessing their lack of concern after assaulting Cole.

She held on to the knife and ran through the trees. She wasn't worried that she might be making too much noise, as the running generators would muffle the sound of her boots crunching over the snow. The only problem was she was leaving a trail even a blind man could follow.

She stopped for a second, got her bearings, and dashed around a covey of brush.

Cole was lying on his back in the snow. It looked like someone had dumped a strawberry icy next to his head. Kate wasn't too concerned by the amount of blood, as she knew head wounds usually bled profusely at first before clotting.

Kneeling beside her husband, Kate shook his shoulder.

"Cole! Wake up!" she said, firmly. She put the knife down and grabbed him by both shoulders and shook him again. "Damn it, Cole!" This time she couldn't hold back the tears. "Don't you die on me!"

Cole opened his eyes. "I'm awake already."

"Oh thank God." Kate leaned down and kissed him.

"What happened?"

"Never mind. We have to go."

"Why are you covered in blood? What'd they do to you?"

"It's not mine."

"Then who..."

"Not now. We can't stay here. Can you stand?"

"Ah, yeah. I think so."

Kate grabbed Cole by the arm and pulled him onto his feet.

He was a little wobbly and felt the back of his head. "Jesus, my head hurts." He looked down at his blood-smeared hand. "Now I remember. Bastard hit me with a shovel."

"Yeah, and that bastard's dead."

"What do you mean?"

"Someone threw a rock and killed him."

"Who?"

"I have no idea. But once they find his body, they're going to come looking for me."

"And *me*."

"I'm pretty sure they think you're dead."

"Sorry to disappoint."

"Come on. We need to get back to our camp, get our stuff, and get the hell out of here."

Kate picked up the knife and let Cole use her as a crutch as they hobbled through the snow. "Wait a second," she said, reaching inside her coat pocket. "Crap."

"What?"

"They took my phone."

Suddenly they both turned and looked back in the direction they'd just come.

"Ah shit!" Cole swore.

"Run!" Kate said.

The generators had stopped.

17

Marcus was happy Josie hadn't been in a big hurry to go back to her house and stayed talking with Libby and entertaining Kaylee with some of her stories about raising animals on the farm. It gave him time to finish up painting the front room. When the fumes got to be too much, everyone went outside on the porch where Duke was lying, enjoying the late afternoon sun. Marcus set up some folding chairs.

So as not to seem inhospitable to their guest, Libby dashed inside and came out with a loaf of bread, deli lunchmeat wrapped in white butcher paper, a packet of sliced cheese, a jar of mustard, some napkins, and a butter knife.

Marcus carried out a cooler filled with canned drinks. He opened the icebox and handed out the beverages then closed the lid so Libby could use the surface for making sandwiches.

"Please forgive us. I hope this is okay? We weren't expecting company," Libby apologized, handing Josie the first sandwich.

"Nonsense, this is wonderful. I hope you didn't mind me just dropping in?"

"No, not at all," Libby said. "I'm glad you did."

Josie popped the tab on her can and took a drink. "It's been a while since I've had a cream soda." A melancholy look came over her face. "This used to be Lewis' favorite."

Marcus thought for sure Josie was going to become forlorn thinking of her deceased husband and ruin their fun get-together, but she didn't. Instead, she gave everyone a big smile and took a bite of her sandwich. She tore off a piece of crust and shared it with Duke.

After they had finished eating, Josie wiped her mouth with a napkin and said, "I really enjoyed that."

"You're so welcome," Libby said.

Josie got up from her chair. "I should get going."

"What, walk back?" Libby glanced over at Marcus.

"It's not far," Josie said.

"Let me drive you," Marcus offered. "It's getting late." The sun was still visible but was steadily sinking behind the treetops.

"Well, thank you, Marcus."

"Can we all go?" Kaylee asked.

"Sure, I'll show you my animals."

Marcus went inside, grabbed his keys, and locked the front door. He went over to the truck and dropped the tailgate. Duke jumped up into the bed of the truck.

"Can I ride in the back with Duke?" Kaylee asked.

"Sure, we're not going very far," Marcus said. He helped his daughter up and she sat next to the big dog. Marcus closed the tailgate and went around to the driver side.

Libby was sitting in the middle of the bench seat, Josie by the passenger door.

"You know the way," Josie said.

Marcus glanced over his shoulder to make sure Kaylee and Duke were situated then started up the truck.

It took Marcus a few minutes to get to Josie's place as he drove slowly, keeping the bumpy ride to a minimal, doing his best to avoid any humps and potholes.

Marcus stopped the truck in front of Josie's farmhouse and they piled out of the cab. He went around and dropped the tailgate. Duke dove out and landed on the ground like a bull coming down off a hill. Kaylee scooted off the tailgate.

He looked around and was amazed at the contrast between the Mills' farm and his grandfather's place. There was a fresh coat of paint on the farmhouse and barn. Each roof looked fairly new.

A small shed was inside a fifty-foot square corral surrounded on all four sides by woven wire fencing. Marcus saw maybe forty goats of different sizes and coloring, some white with black heads, grazing on hay strewn upon the ground.

A chicken coop the size of a one-car garage was in the middle of the two buildings. The structure was well made with weather treated lumber and galvanized steel wire with the same size hexagon gaps—unlike his grandfather's nightmarish creation. Rough count there had to be over thirty chickens.

Libby and Kaylee walked over to look at the goats.

Marcus caught Josie out of the corner of his eye, watching him stare at the chicken coop.

"You know, Marcus, you could do me a big favor."

"Oh, what's that?"

"Well, Lewis was never one to figure out a job proper. Always bought more than he needed. How would you like to take some of it off my hands? It's all in the barn."

"I'd pay you," Marcus said.

"No need. I really have no use for it."

"Thanks, Josie."

"It's what neighbors do."

Kaylee screamed.

Marcus saw his daughter pointing at a goat that was lying on the ground. Libby was peering over the fence. He turned to Josie and was surprised to see a big grin on her face. He followed Josie over to the corral.

"Oh my God, Marcus. We were just looking at the goats when this one just keeled over," Libby said.

"Is it dead?" Kaylee asked.

"No, it's quite all right," Josie said. "You must have startled it. That's a myotonic goat."

"A what?" Libby asked.

"A fainting goat. As soon as they feel threatened their leg muscles freeze up and they topple over. It's quite comical."

"Scared me," Kaylee confessed.

"You needn't worry." Josie opened the gate and walked inside the pen. She went down on one knee and stroked the goat's side. Like magic, the goat *'came back to life'* and got on its feet.

"Do they all do that?" Libby asked.

"No, fortunately."

"It's almost like an epileptic seizure," Marcus said.

"Somewhat," Josie said. "The technical term of the condition is *myotonia congenita*."

"How strange," Libby said.

Josie stepped out of the goat pen and closed the gate. She led everyone over to the chicken coop and opened the door to the enclosure. "Come on in." The ceiling was high enough so that no one had to stoop, not even Marcus. There were perches on three walls for the chickens to lay their eggs.

"Are you considering getting any chickens?" Josie asked as she waded through the fowl pecking at the ground.

"Well..." Libby looked at Marcus and he shrugged his shoulders.

"Can we?" Kaylee gazed up at Marcus.

"Sure, why not."

"What would you suggest?"

"Depends on what type of chicken you're looking for."

"Eggs would be nice," Libby said. "I don't think I could raise one and..." Libby mouthed the words 'kill it' so Kaylee couldn't hear.

"Some chickens make excellent pets."

"I want one." Kaylee gazed once again at Marcus with those sad eyes of hers.

"I'm sure there's a lot to consider."

Marcus could tell that Libby wasn't quite sold on the idea. Even he had a difficult time imagining a chicken roaming about their house like a pet cat.

"What would you recommend, egg-wise?" Libby asked.

Josie glanced around and spotted a chicken with a light-colored body and black rump. She scooped it off the ground and held it like a small dog in the crook of her arm.

"This breed is an Araucana. This one is perfect for Easter as it lays blue eggs."

"Blue eggs?" Kaylee laughed. "That's cool."

"She's very good natured and would make an excellent pet."

"We could call her Bunny," Kaylee said.

"What, like the Easter bunny?" Marcus said. "It's a chicken, not a rabbit."

"I know that."

Marcus knew his head would explode trying to understand his daughter's logic.

"If it's quantity you're looking for, I do have some leghorns," Josie said, pointing to a congregation of white-feathered chickens with pointy rustic-red combs and waddles under their beaks. "If you were to take, say, half a dozen it would sure help me cut down on my feed cost."

"How much?"

"You'd be doing me a service. No charge."

Marcus looked at Libby. "Well, I guess now we're officially farmers."

18

Avery was about to turn down the drive to Josie's house when he spotted a truck parked in her yard and a young man and woman with a little girl talking with Josie. He wasn't quite sure who they were but by the way they were acting, it seemed like they were having a friendly visit. Even though he wanted desperately to alert Josie of the possible danger he thought he should wait, as he didn't want to impose.

He kept driving, figuring to drop by later. It would have felt weird—at least to him—to show up, especially in uniform, and interrupt Josie and her guests.

There was so much he wanted to tell her. How he felt. The nights he'd lay awake, thinking about her and what it would be like if they were together. But each time the fantasy played out in his head, so did the guilt knowing that she was Lewis' wife. Even though her husband was dead and buried, it still seemed like he was cheating on his friend.

He tried to put it all out of his mind, and after a fifteen minute drive further up the mountain, he arrived at Weston Eggers' chalet, which looked more like a hunting lodge as there were bear skins pinned on the walls along with mounted elk racks and deer antlers.

Weston was a renowned trapper and hunter. Ranchers and farmers hired him whenever they had problems with coyotes and mountain lions killing their livestock. He was known to hide out in the bushes in his camouflaged ghillie suit for hours on end waiting for the culprit to show up then drop it with his high-powered rifle.

As Weston's home was at a slightly higher elevation, there was more snow on the ground and in the trees.

Avery was about to go up the steps when the door opened and Weston came out to greet him.

"Hey, Avery. What do I owe the honors?"

"Been over at the Cobb's farm. Seems something attacked their sheep."

"Any idea what it was?"

Avery avoided the question. Instead, he said, "How long have we known each other?"

"I don't know, fifteen years."

"That'd be about right. Ever know me to exaggerate?"

"You mean besides your fish stories?"

Avery nodded.

"I reckon not."

"Then if I tell you something, you promise you won't think I'm—"

"Exaggerating, yeah I get it."

"We found a Bigfoot track."

Weston gave Avery an incredulous look. "Bigfoot?"

"That's right."

"And where was this?"

"A short distance up from the Cobb's farm. Maybe a mile, there's a rock shelf."

"I know the spot," Weston said. "I have a line of traps back up in there."

"When's the last time you checked them?"

"A couple days ago."

"You planning on going up there soon?"

"Thought I'd go up tomorrow."

"Then I'd be very careful," Avery said.

"You seriously think it was a Bigfoot. I mean, when's the last time you even saw one?"

"You know the answer to that."

"Never, am I wrong?"

Avery liked Weston but sometimes the man could be exasperating. He frowned and shook his head.

"That's because the damn things don't exist," Weston said flatly. "I should know, I've been hunting and trapping this mountain for the best part of twenty years and I've never seen one. If you ask me, it was probably a cougar hungry for a good lamb stew."

"You can make light of it if you want, but I know what I saw. Just thought you should know."

"Thanks for the heads up," Weston grinned.

Avery got in the Bronco and headed back to the main road. He was about to turn left when a mail truck drove up, turned, and parked beside him. The driver rolled down the window. "Evening, Sheriff."

"Working a little late, aren't we?"

Rhett Sawyer had been the local mail carrier for more years than Avery could count. The Postal Service figured it better keep the old-timer around, as he was the only one that knew where all the residents lived; no matter how inaccessible and obscure their addresses were.

Avery figured he must be rich, tucking it away collecting a pension, wages, and Social Security. But none of that seemed to matter. The man just loved his job.

"I'm almost done," Rhett said. "Two more stops."

"I'd be careful out there."

"Why, did someone spot some mail thieves?"

"No, nothing like that. There's a dangerous animal out there. Just wanted you to know."

"Thanks, I'll keep my eyes open. If I see anything suspicious I'll be sure to give you a call."

"You do that." Avery drove off. He figured he'd give it another hour then swing by Josie's, tell her to keep a watchful eye on her animals, that there was a predator roaming the mountain.

Who knows, she might even ask him to stay.

19

They'd been searching the woods in the dark. Boyd was the first to find Seth. He yelled out and Red and Jesse came running over.

Boyd shone his flashlight on the body.

"Jesus, his damn head," Jesse said. "Looks like a bashed-in gourd."

"There's the rock she used," Boyd said, shining the beam on the bloody cobblestone lying a couple feet away in the snow.

"Pretty feisty for a little thing," Red said, holding the short-barrel scattergun at his side.

Boyd and Jesse were armed as well. Boyd had removed his waders and had a semi-automatic pistol tucked in his belt. The wood grain handgrip of a revolver stuck out of the front of Jesse's jeans.

"What do you want to do?" Boyd asked Red.

"Leave him."

"Aren't we going to bury him?" Jesse asked.

"Be my guest," Red said.

"Good luck digging a grave," Boyd said. "This ground is nothing but shale."

"Shouldn't we say something?"

"Like what?" Boyd asked.

"Some words, like a preacher."

"Okay," Red said. "How about thank you very much you stupid bastard for getting yourself killed and giving us a three-way split?"

"That's it?" Jesse asked.

"Unless you have something you want to add?"

"Nah."

"What about her?" Boyd panned his light on the footprints leading into the trees.

"Well, I doubt she's gone far."

Boyd led the way and they followed the tracks in the snow. The trail angled behind a hedge of shrubs where there was a large impression in the snow with a blotch of blood.

"I thought you said he was dead?" Red glared at Jesse in the dim light.

"You saw it. Seth nearly took his head off."

"Now there's two to worry about," Boyd said.

"They must have a camp somewhere," Red said.

"So we follow them?"

"We will. But first, we need to move our equipment out of sight. I don't want anyone else stumbling on to our little operation."

"You're not worried they'll get away?" Boyd asked.

"Look at those tracks."

Boyd shone his light on the ground. Each impression was superimposed by another, suggesting that one person was helping the other stagger through the snow.

"They won't be hard to find."

***

Cole had a world-class headache but he refused to stop. It was difficult to see in the shadowy trees. He glanced up through the branches and saw a sliver of moon and figured once they were out of the woods they might be able to see better. He could hear rushing water to his right.

"We're almost to the creek."

They stepped out between the trees.

Cole could see the glittering stream and the snowy bank in the faint moonlight.

Up above, the starless night sky bulged with the next storm front.

Cole recognized the shoreline and knew this was the correct way back to their camp. He looked over his shoulder expecting to see Red with his shotgun and the other two, but there was no one following them.

"There's our campsite," Kate said. She went over to the edge of the water and washed the blood from her face. She took off her parka and rubbed the blood-soaked material in the snow to remove some of the stain but not too much that the coat would be too wet to wear. She put her jacket back on and rushed over to join Cole by the tent.

"Grab your backpack," Cole said. "We'll leave the tent and sleeping bags."

Kate reached inside the dome tent and pulled out both packs. They scrambled to grab what they could and stuffed their bags.

"Here, put this on," Cole said, handing Kate a headlamp with straps. She slipped it over her hair and turned on the small LED light, which shone directly into Cole's face.

"Not yet, turn it off! Before they see it."

Kate switched off the light.

Cole looked around and spotted what could be the trail in the trees but it was difficult to be sure with all the snow. "Ah, I think it was through there." He started to traipse over to the trees but then stopped and glanced back at the ground.

Kate stared down at Cole's footprints. "We might as well leave a string of flares."

Cole stared up at the mountain. "There's no way we're going to get over that and find our way in the snow. We're lost without the GPS."

"What other way is there?"

"We'll hike downstream. Lose them on the rocks."

"You really think that's a good idea?"

"Kate, trust me. Besides, they always say sooner or later if you follow water you're going to run into someone."

"Our luck, it'll be those assholes' second cousins."

"Let's head out. Once we round that bend, we'll switch on our lights."

20

Kaine Brown made sure he had plenty of ventilation inside the equipment shed by leaving the back entrance and one of the big front doors open wide enough to create a cross draft. Operating a moonshine still indoors was always risky as too much heat could over-pressurize the pot and cause it to explode, so it meant keeping the interior of the shed as cool as possible even if it meant freezing his ass off.

Kaine's grandfather had almost died in one such accident and he'd always kept his boiler out in the woods.

But Kaine had his own way of doing things. Always had. Which was the reason he'd dropped out of school before he was sixteen. He'd lied about his age and gone into the Army. Hadn't been in for more than five months before they booted him out. That's when he thought he knew everything.

He was so cocksure that he could get away with anything, he committed armed robbery and got caught running away through a field. He served three years in a federal prison. Would have been a twenty-year stretch if they'd found the gun he'd tossed into an irrigation ditch filled with water.

After he got out, he swore he'd never take orders from anyone again, which was why he never stayed gainfully employed. But as luck would have it, he learned he had a knack for moonshine. It was in his blood. Passed down to him by his long-deceased granddaddy.

Four days ago he had boiled up sacks of cornmeal, sugar, water, and yeast and let it ferment into mash. He added the pulpous mush to the copper pot, which was resting on a steel grate over a wood-burning pit. The fire was so hot, the flames were licking up through the blackened bars. Living in the forest there was always an endless supply of fuel, and it was free, which drastically reduced his operation costs and excelled his profit margin whenever he wasn't using a propane tank.

Kaine had a steady flow of loyal customers and business was booming. And if they brought along their own empty Mason jar, he'd even knock off a couple bucks.

But now the sheriff was out to get him. He knew if Avery Anderson said he was going to pay him a visit everyday then that's exactly what he was going to do, and that would eventually put him out of business. No one was going to buy hooch from a moonshiner that had the law breathing down his neck.

And all because of that damn dog.

He could hear it outside.

Whimpering in the cold.

He was tempted to go out and shoot it, put it out of its misery, but that would be a kindness, and right now, he was pissed as hell and enjoyed listening to it suffer.

He stepped around the massive five-foot tall copper boiler making sure not to get too close to the flames and catch his pant leg on fire. He checked the fittings on the long copper piping and the condensation coils for leaks. He could hear the steady drip as vapor condensed into liquid and filled the collector.

Six wooden boxes—each with nine jars of 190-proof pure grain alcohol—were on the ground next to the wall of shelves stocked with Mason jars filled with precisely the same amount of spirits. Most of the jars were already labeled with a specific number that corresponded with a customer's name—a code only Kaine knew.

An icy breeze blew into the building, causing the light fixture hanging down from the ceiling by the door to sway.

Kaine shivered and rolled his shirtsleeves down and buttoned the cuffs. If it got any colder he would have to go back inside the cabin and fetch his jacket.

A huge shadow loomed over the wall of shelves.

Kaine slowly turned around.

And saw a giant creature bump its head against the light shade, which meant that it had to be eight feet tall. In the shadows it looked like a massive man but when the light bulb shined back on it, Kaine could see that it wasn't human. It had broad shoulders and a barrel chest with thick arms and legs and monstrous five-fingered hands. It was covered in grayish-red hair from head to foot, and even under all that fur, he could tell the animal was extremely muscular and had to be unbelievably strong.

Its head was covered with the same texture of hair like its body except for the upper parts of its leathery-skinned face. The eyes were big black orbs sunken under a furrowing brow, the nose flattened with flaring nostrils. Its mouth hung open, revealing yellow chipped and jagged tombstone-shaped teeth.

Even though he had never seen one before, Kaine knew he was standing only ten feet away from an actual Bigfoot.

Holy Jesus, they are real!

Even though he was scared shitless, he couldn't help thinking how rich he'd be if he were to kill this thing. Hell, he'd be famous. But it would take more than a few bullets to bring it down.

That is, unless he got it dead between the eyes. Even a thick skull like that couldn't stop a .38 caliber bullet to the brainpan.

Kaine looked up and his eyes met with the creature's. So far, it hadn't budged or made a sound. As though it was waiting for Kaine to make the first move. Like two gunfighters sizing each other up before the draw.

He kept staring at the Bigfoot making sure their eyes were locked so it wouldn't notice him reaching slyly for his gun. No sudden movement, nice and slow. His fingers closed around the handgrip of the Taurus. One quick pull and he'd get off a shot and drop it where it stood. Hell, he'd practiced enough shooting cans off a stump. Only then he'd been thinking he might one day have a showdown with a dissatisfied customer or someone trying to break in and steal his moonshine.

Not a damn Bigfoot.

He inched his forefinger into the trigger guard.

Felt the trigger press into the crook of his finger.

His gaze was unwavering.

The Bigfoot glanced down at the gun.

Kaine yanked the revolver out of the holster, but before he could point and shoot, the Bigfoot had closed the ten-foot gap between them and slammed its fist into his chest.

The blow punched him off his feet and sent him flying back into the shelves of Mason jars. His head and shirt were drenched with clear alcohol as the glass shattered all around him and the shelving crashed down. He could feel sharp shards deep in his back.

He slumped on the ground and saw that his gun had flown clear across the dirt floor to the other side of the shed. He reached out to pull himself up. He jerked his hand away when he realized he had just touched the red-hot grate under the boiler.

His hand was on fire.

A crackling flame ran up his shirtsleeve and spread onto the front of his alcohol-drenched shirt.

"Aaahhhh!" he screamed as he tried to put the fire out with his other hand. He watched in horror as his fingers ignited and his hand became a fiery torch. He looked up expecting to see the Bigfoot but the animal had fled.

It wasn't until the flames spread down to his legs that he knew if he wanted to remain alive he would have to run outside and roll in the snow, but as he started for the doorway his head became engulfed.

He staggered out, his entire body ablaze. He couldn't scream because his vocal cords were seared. His face was scorched and he could only see out of one eye. He took two more steps and fell on the ground, his charred body sizzling in the snow as he rolled over on his back.

He was in extreme agony, a million pinpricks of pain shooting through every pore of his body.

He could hear crunching in the snow and turned his head. His vision was blurry in his one eye but there was no mistaking what it was.

It was the damn dog.

Creeping toward him.

The dog came closer and sniffed Kaine's burnt face.

Go away you miserable mutt!

A dry, raspy tongue licked his charred flesh.

I can't believe it. Even after the way I tortured and mistreated it, it still forgives me. So it is true, and not some bullshit, that thing about unconditional love. Well, isn't this...

Kaine felt a tug and the back of his head lifted off the snow.

Oh, God, the damn dog's eating me!

21

Cole and Kate followed the shoreline down the creek. It was tricky crossing the rocks in the dark even with their headlamps. Each time Cole stepped ahead in front of Kate, his body would block her light and cast a big shadow. Twice he had misjudged his step and almost twisted an ankle. They'd been hiking for almost two hours and had no idea how far they had traveled. The trek had been slow crossing over the rugged terrain and it had begun to snow, light flurries at first then heavier snowflakes, but nowhere near a category blizzard.

"We should find a place to hide out for the night," Kate said, her voice strained and her breathing winded.

"You sure you don't want to keep going?" Even though Cole was tired and his feet were killing him, he didn't think it would be wise to stop. For all he knew, they were not too far behind, picking up their trail. There was no way he'd be able to sleep wondering if he would wake up to a gun muzzle pressed in his face.

"Cole, I'm about to drop."

"Okay, then." He crossed over a boulder and peered into the nearby trees. There was some shrubbery they could camp behind so that they wouldn't be seen from the creek. "Let's go back in there," Cole said, and led the way through the coppice to a small clearing in the trees.

They took a minute to take off their backpacks and got out what they needed before turning off their headlamps. There was enough moonlight for them to grope around in the dark and perform simple tasks.

Cole had laid out a ground cloth for them to sit on. He took their other ground cloth and stretched it between two tree trunks with some rope to form a lean-to to shield them from the snow while Kate set up the small cook stove.

She put some snow in a pot and placed it on the burner. It quickly boiled into water. Kate added a packet of powdered chicken noodle soup.

"Hmm, that smells good," Cole said, realizing that they hadn't eaten anything the entire day.

"I know I'm a wonderful cook," Kate said.

"You could have your own network show. 'Kate Wagner's Cooking Tips.'"

"Yeah, imagine me standing in front of a live studio audience demonstrating my culinary skills boiling this shit."

Cole put his arm around Kate. "Don't worry, we'll get out of this."

"You know, I really thought that bastard was going to kill me."

"Yeah, but he didn't."

"I still don't know what really happened." Kate poured the soup from the pot into two aluminum mugs.

"I think it was their leader, Red," Cole said.

"Why do you say that?"

"Maybe he wanted you all for himself." Cole blew on his soup and took a sip.

"I don't think it was him. He didn't seem that interested. My guess it was either Bob or Jason."

"I think their names were Boyd and Jesse."

"Whatever."

"Or maybe it wasn't about you."

"What, you don't think they found me attractive?"

"Sure, but what if it was about the gold. You saw the nuggets; there was a fortune there." Cole drank some soup.

"What about it?"

"With one of them out of the way, there'd be more to go around."

"Now I get what you're saying. So they weren't horny just greedy."

"Doesn't that make you feel better?"

"Not really. Not what you call an ego booster."

Cole finished his cup.

Kate drank half and placed her cup on the ground. "We should try and get some sleep."

"You go first. I'll stay up and keep watch."

"Wake me up after a couple of hours and I'll take my turn."

"You got it."

Kate huddled to stay warm and curled up in a fetus position on the ground cloth and was soon fast asleep.

Cole rested his back against the tree trunk and sat cross-legged with the knife by his side.

He wished they hadn't been in such a panic and had taken the time to break down the dome tent and roll up the sleeping bags and brought them along as it was going to be a cold and miserable night without them.

He also wished he had never confronted Red and his men and seen all that gold.

There was no way they were going to get off this mountain alive.

22

Marcus had a big day planned and got up at daybreak. He crawled out of bed making sure not to wake Libby and quietly got dressed. He slipped on his coat and work gloves and went outside. He could tell right away it had snowed during the night. The hood, top of the cab, and the camper shell on his truck were covered in three inches of snow.

He still had the building supplies in the back of his truck that Josie had given him and wanted to get an early start tearing down the old chicken coop and erecting the new structure. He opened the tailgate and pulled out three tight rolls of galvanized wire fencing and placed them on the ground.

Marcus then dragged out short stacks of two-by-fours, three at a time. Next he took out four-by-eight foot sheets of plywood and some board planks. The exterior wood had already been treated with creosote so it wouldn't rot.

Josie had also given him aluminum roofing that he offloaded last.

He knew later he would have to find a way to thank Josie for her generosity, as he would have easily spent close to three hundred dollars if he'd gone to a hardware store and lumberyard.

Marcus could hear the chickens clucking in the barn. Josie had been kind enough to loan Marcus a couple of carrying cages to transport the birds. Besides the six leghorns, she had also thrown in two more Araucana chickens; one that could lay green eggs, the other pink, which made Kaylee ecstatic.

With a claw hammer and pry bar, Marcus spent half an hour yanking out nails and ripping down parts of the old coop. He was pleased to find that the posts in the ground were solid and hadn't rotted or been damaged by termites, and the back wall with the roosts was sound enough to leave up, which made the job of putting the new structure together easier.

He made three trips using the wheelbarrow carting off the doors, brittle Fiberglas panels, and the kinked chicken wire over to the junk pile. Normally, it would have been unsightly but with all the snow it looked like a sculptor's weird piece of art.

He got to work and began nailing up the framing for the plywood walls.

"Marcus, it's not even seven in the morning," Libby hollered from the porch. She stood sleepy-eyed in her housecoat and slippers with her arms clamped around her chest, shivering.

"Sorry," Marcus shouted back. "I really wanted to get started on this."

"So early?"

"Lib, when you live in the country you're expected to get up before the crack of dawn."

"Oh, really. And who told you that?"

"It's just common knowledge. Ask anyone."

Rather than get into a debate, Libby turned and waved her hand over her head in a dismissive fashion and shuffled back inside the house.

"And no fair going back to bed!" Marcus shouted with a big grin.

23

Avery hadn't slept well thinking about Josie and decided to get an early start and go out on patrol. He had a different route he would take depending on the day of the week so he could cover all of the territory under his jurisdiction, but would always make sure he either began or ended up passing by Josie's place. Today he decided to start at her husband's memorial and swing up the road to warn some more residents that there was a dangerous animal roaming the mountain.

When he reached the tree, he noticed that the ribbon had been removed and the vase of flowers was gone along with the photograph.

Had she given up on her vigil?

Or had some hooligans kicked the memorial over the edge of the cliff?

Could it be that she was no longer pining for Lewis?

Had she decided it was high time she moved on?

Whatever the reason, Avery suddenly felt a swell of hope. He checked the clock on the dashboard. It was 7:45. She'd probably been up before sunrise so it wasn't too early to be showing up on her porch. He put the Bronco into gear, went down the road, and turned in the Mills' driveway.

Josie was tending to her goats when Avery pulled up. He left his hat on the passenger seat and stepped out of his truck.

"Morning, Avery," Josie said over the fence as she scattered grain on the ground that had been cleared of snow so the goats could feed. She laid the bucket down and came out of the stockade.

"Morning," Avery greeted. "Thought I'd drop by to see if you were okay."

"Why wouldn't I be?"

"I saw Lewis' memorial was gone," Avery said.

"Oh, that. I decided it was time to take it down before everyone started calling me the sad grieving widow. I don't think folks paid much attention to it anyway."

"We all miss Lewis. And Ray."

"Care for some coffee?"

"I think I have time. Something I'd like to talk to you about."

Josie gave Avery a smile and went up the porch steps. She opened the screen door and Avery followed her inside. They went into the kitchen.

"Please, have a seat," Josie said.

Avery pulled out a chair and sat down.

Josie grabbed a coffee pot off the wood burning stove, poured the hot brew into two mugs on the drain board, put the coffee pot back on the stovetop, and carried the steaming mugs over to the kitchen table.

Josie sat down. "So, what is it you wanted to tell me?"

Avery gazed over the table, and for a moment he thought he might just blurt it out, tell her how he felt about her, but instead he said, "Lou and Arlene lost a couple of sheep to a predator."

"What kind of predator?" Josie asked, and took a sip of her coffee.

"Well, that's the thing." Avery took a moment to take a drink and stared down at his mug.

"Avery, what is it? You're not hiding something from me are you? Whatever it is, I'd like to know."

Avery didn't want to scare Josie and hated to lie to her, but he wasn't sure how she would react if he told her the truth. There was only one way to find out and that was just to say it.

"Okay, don't laugh, but Lou and I think it's a Bigfoot."

"Did you say Bigfoot?" Josie gave Avery an incredulous look.

"Now, I don't want you to worry—"

"Really, Avery? A Bigfoot?" Josie leaned back from the table and broke out laughing.

"Josie, I think you need to take this seriously."

"A bobcat or a cougar, I would believe, but a Bigfoot? I'm sorry, Avery. Don't tell me Lou keeps a bottle out in his shearing shed."

"I know it sounds farfetched but you should have seen the footprint, it was huge."

"Sure you two weren't stepping over each others' tracks?"

"Josie!" Avery snapped, a little louder than he intended.

Why wouldn't she take him seriously? No, they hadn't trod in the same imprint. Had they? Was this how she thought of him, some buffoon wearing a sheriff's badge.

"I appreciate you coming by and telling me, but I really have to get back to my goats." Josie got up from the table, but was no longer smiling. She grabbed her mug, went over to the sink, and poured the rest of her coffee down the drain.

"Yeah, I better get going." Avery stood, but left his mug on the table. "I'll see my way out." He turned without saying goodbye, leaving the kitchen, and strode across the front room.

He walked out the front door cursing himself under his breath as he made his way to the Bronco.

When he got in and started the engine to drive off, he half-expected Josie to be standing on her porch, but he was sadly disappointed, as she hadn't bothered to follow him out of the house.

24

Boyd lifted one pontoon while Jesse held up the other pontoon and they carried the bulky dredge and sluice into the trees. They placed it next to the tumbler and the rest of their hand tools and buckets that they had moved earlier. They grabbed a large camouflage netting and covered the equipment so that it wasn't visible from the creek.

Boyd even took some handfuls of snow and sprinkled them over the cover to make it appear more natural like the snow that had fallen during the night disguising the quarried ground the men had dug up.

"You boys thirsty?" Red tipped the Mason jar to his lips, took a swig and swallowed then inhaled deeply as the 190-proof alcohol burned his gullet.

"I'll take some of that," Boyd said and Red passed him the jar. He took a gulp and made a face and handed it over to Jesse. After Jesse took his turn, he gave the jar back to Red.

They passed the high-octane moonshine around two more times.

"I have to hand it to Kaine; he sure knows how to make a mean batch of shine," Jesse said. He went to hand the jar over to Red and almost fumbled it, spilling some in the snow.

"That's enough," Red said, snatching the jar and screwing on the lid. He held up the near empty jar. "We're going to have to pay Kaine a visit pretty soon. Get us stocked up. But first, we have some hunting to do."

They trudged through the snow pack and around a boulder where they had their utility all terrain 4-wheelers with short flat cargo beds, stashed out of sight. Each quad bike had large knobby mud and snow tires and was designed for maneuvering on either dry land or muddy conditions.

"If this weather keeps up we might have to break out the Ski-Doos," Jesse said, hopping on the seat of his quad.

"Still think we should have gone after them last night," Boyd said, seated behind his handlebars.

"What and slept out here freezing our tails off, no way," Jesse said, decidedly grateful that Red had opted they hold up for the night back at their cabin, which wasn't more than a couple miles away back in the forest.

"They couldn't have gotten far," Red said. "Besides, Jesse here has the nose of a bloodhound. Ain't that right, Jessie boy?"

"They could be sitting up in some damn tree and I'd find them."

"Then lead the way."

The men hit the starter buttons and revved up the four-stroke engines.

Jesse took off first, kicking up mud and snow as he headed off into the trees, Red and Boyd close behind.

It didn't take them long before they reached the abandoned campsite.

Boyd dismounted while the other two men remained on their quads. He walked around, checking out what was left behind. He peeked inside the tent. "Their sleeping bags are still here. And some clothes."

"Maybe they never came back," Red said.

"Yeah, then where are their backpacks?" Boyd said. "They wouldn't have come all the way out here without backpacks."

"They must have been in a mighty big hurry to leave their gear behind," Jesse said.

"Scared, is more like it." Red looked up the steep mountain teeming with snow and turned to Jesse. "There's no way they would have tackled that in the dark."

"Yeah, that guy's probably half dead the way Seth hit him with that shovel. They're going to stick to flat ground." Jesse glanced downstream. "I'll bet they follow the creek."

"Then that's what we'll do."

"I say we split up," Boyd said. "That way we'll cover more area. If one of us spot them, just fire a shot."

"I agree. Jesse, you take this side. Boyd and I will cross over, just in case they try to sneak across."

"Don't worry, they're not going to fool this bird dog," Jesse grinned.

Red and Boyd fired up their bikes and headed for the creek. They held on tight to their handlebars and bounced across the rocky stream.

Jesse gunned his quad and raced down the shoreline.

25

Early morning sunlight was filtering down through the trees when Cole suddenly opened his eyes and found himself still sitting with his back up against the tree. He knew instantly he had drifted off sometime in the night without waking Kate.

He glanced over and saw Kate fast asleep on the ground cloth. He gave her a nudge. "Kate! Wake up!"

She squinted up at him. "Is it time?"

"Time for us to go."

"Wait a minute; it's already light? I was supposed to relieve you. Why didn't you wake me?"

"I fell asleep," Cole confessed. He managed to get on his feet even though his back felt like he'd slept the night on a bed of nails.

"Sleeping on watch is a court marshal offense."

"Then throw me in the brig. I guess I was more tired than I thought. Getting hit over the head will do that."

"How is your head?"

"Still throbs a little but not like yesterday. Better hurry it up," Cole said. He broke down the lean-to and gathered up both ground cloths. He slipped on his backpack, and when Kate stood, he helped her put on her backpack.

"How far down do you think we'll have to go?" she asked.

"I forgot the name but I remember seeing a small town on the map not too far from Diamondback River. If we find a shallow spot, we can cut across the creek, follow it down till we reach the river and look for the town."

Cole and Kate started down the snowy bank and headed downstream.

They'd hike for almost an hour when they came to an L-shaped bend in the creek where a rockslide had partially dammed the waterway creating a stepping stone pathway across, but also causing a more turbulent current. One false step and the fast moving water would sweep them off their feet.

"I think we should try here," Cole said.

"I don't know, Cole. It doesn't look very safe."

"We're going to have to get across sooner or later."

"Maybe we should—" Kate turned to a droning sound off in the distance. "What is that?"

"Sounds like a motorbike or one of those ATVs."

"It's them isn't it?"

"Come on." Cole trudged through the snow to the water's edge. He stomped his boots on the rocks to dislodge any ice from the rubber-sole treads. He didn't see any green moss but knew the rocks would be slippery. He raised his arms out from his sides for balance and stepped out on the first rock. Making sure his footing was sound, he stretched out to the next rock. "Just follow my lead, and you'll be okay," he called over his shoulder.

The easy part was treading over the rocks that had formed the barrier restricting the natural flow of the stream; the real challenge was making it the rest of the way where the swift current splashed through the boulders, making the stony surfaces slick and treacherous to cross.

Twice, Cole's boots almost went out from under him, but he quickly caught himself and regained his balance. He kept going, giving Kate a pep talk as they went along. He was afraid to look back to see if she was okay for fear of losing his concentration and falling in the water. As he neared the opposite shore, the raging water became louder.

Cole made it to the other side, jumped onto the snowy bank, and turned around.

Kate was standing indecisive, contemplating her next move from where she stood to the next rock. Cole remembered that same spot, that he had to leap across, as it was a considerable gap. Now he wondered if it was too wide for Kate to cross.

He could hear the faint sound of engines off in the forest.

"Kate! Just go for it!" he yelled.

She took a step back, gathering up the nerve then leapt to the next boulder.

Instead of landing on her feet, she slipped, and fell on her face and chest. She clawed at the rock and stopped herself from sliding into the water. Gradually, she pulled herself up and got back on her feet. She continued on and managed to get across without further incident. She hopped off the last rock into Cole's waiting arms.

"Well, that wasn't exactly graceful," he said.

"Shut up, I hit my chin. Hurts like the dickens."

The abrasion on her chin was weeping a little blood.

"Looks like you got in a fight with a cheese grater."

"Very funny."

Cole glanced down the fast moving stream and could see where the headwaters flowed into the whitewater rapids of the Diamondback River.

He turned and saw a snowy slope that looked like it wouldn't be too difficult to hike up. The higher elevation would give them a clearer view of the terrain ahead and maybe they could spot the town Cole had seen on the map.

"You go first," Cole said and let Kate take the lead so he could assist her if she had trouble getting up the incline.

They spent the next ten minutes climbing the snowy embankment and came upon the backside of a small building.

"What is that?" Kate asked, examining the crude structure.

"Looks like a shed."

"The door's open."

Cole approached first. He stood at the doorway and peeked inside. "Do you smell that?"

"Smells like a brewery," Kate answered.

"Holy cow," Cole said and stepped inside. "It's a damn distillery."

Kate followed him in. "What's with all the broken bottles?"

"Looks like someone ransacked the place." Cole went over to the shelf and found a jar that wasn't broken. He unscrewed the lid and took a whiff of the contents. "Whoa, that's some strong shit." Cole held the jar out for Kate to smell.

"My God," Kate said, turning away after taking a sniff.

"Want to try some?"

"Cole, don't you think we're in enough trouble?"

"But this is moonshine. The Real McCoy."

"Made by Hatfield hillbilly crazies!"

"Not even a sip?"

"Hell, after the day we've had, sure why not."

Cole raised the jar to his lips and took a gulp. He turned his head, coughed, and managed to say, "Smooth," then handed the jar to Kate.

She took a fair-sized drink, swallowed, and smiled. "Cole, you're such a lightweight." She took the lid from Cole and screwed the lid back on and put the jar back on the shelf. "There, no one will even know we were ever here."

"Let's hope not." Cole walked by the big boiler. He strode out through the large front door and saw the cabin across the yard. "Hey, we're in luck. Maybe there's someone inside."

"I don't know Cole. There's something not right about this place." Kate walked up beside Cole and looked to her left. "Holy shit!"

"What?"

"My God, there's someone in that crate!"

Cole glanced over and saw a charred arm protruding out of the open end of a large wooden box most likely used for shipping equipment parts.

The blackened arm was moving up and down as if trying to attract their attention.

"Hey, you okay?" Cole called out, traipsing through the snow toward the crate.

"Are you hurt?" Kate asked, walking beside Cole. "My God, Cole. Look at his arm. Must have been caught in a fire."

"Let us help you." Cole got close enough and bent down to get a better look at who was inside the crate.

And that's when he saw the two bloodshot eyes peering out of the gloom and the snarling teeth.

"Jesus, Kate! Watch out!" Cole stepped back and bumped into Kate.

Just as a vicious mongrel dog poked its head out of the crate, holding a severed arm in its jaws.

Cole made sure they were far enough way from the menacing dog before he turned around. He could see portions of a burn victim lying under the snow. "The rest of the body is over there."

"What the hell happened here?" Kate gasped.

"Who knows? We better see if anyone's in the cabin."

Cole went up to the front door and knocked. When no one answered, he turned the knob and opened the door. "Anyone inside?"

Again, there was no answer.

Cole stepped inside. The interior was rustic with plank flooring and actual log- and mud-jointed walls. There were two 4-pane windows, each partially covered with black plastic garbage bags, in the front on either side of the only door that led into the cabin. A pillow and rumpled blanket were on a bed up against one wall. Three wood chairs and a small table for eating, a wood-burning stove and icebox and some incidentals.

Not much of anything else.

Except what appeared to be an assortment of gun parts strewn on the tabletop.

Cole looked at the menagerie and figured there were three semiautomatic handguns that someone—most likely the poor soul out there in the snow—had been in the process of field stripping and never got the chance to reassemble.

"Ever put one of these together?" Kate asked, gazing down at the table.

"Yeah, once with my brother's gun and an instruction sheet."

26

Kaylee was helping her mother with the baking when she heard her father open the front door and come into the house. She got so excited she dropped her wooden stirring spoon on the table, missing the bowl of cake batter, and dashed through the kitchen.

"Kaylee, look at the mess you made," her mother scolded, but Kaylee had already run off into the front room.

"Is it done, Daddy?"

"I've a few finishing touches, but yes, it's about done. I went ahead and moved the chickens into their new home."

Kaylee turned when her mother came in the room. She was expecting her to be mad, but instead she put on a big smile. "Marcus, seriously, you've already completed the chicken coop? I'm impressed."

"Guess I found my true calling."

"Can I go see?" Kaylee asked.

"Sure, as long as you follow one basic rule," her father said.

Kaylee knew her dad was a stickler when it came to rules...

Better pick up your room or no TV or *Finish your plate or no dessert* or *No bedtime story until you brush your teeth.*

"What rule is that, Daddy?"

"When you go into their run, always make sure you close the gate after yourself, or the chickens will get out and run away."

"That's it?"

"That's it. Think you can remember to always do that?"

"Always close the gate."

"Good, you got it."

"I'm going to see if Bunny laid an egg," Kaylee shouted and ran for the front door.

"Whoa there! Not so fast," her father shouted.

Kaylee stopped and turned around.

"Didn't you forget something?"

"What? Oh, thank you, Daddy."

"Well, you're welcome. But there's something else."

Kaylee gave her father a puzzled look then suddenly realized he was holding something behind his back.

He reached around and held up his hand. "You can't gather eggs unless you have a basket."

Kaylee ran up to her father and gave him a quick hug then snatched the basket by the handle and charged across the room.

"Don't break any," her father called out, but by then she was already out the door and running down the porch steps to the snow-covered yard.

Her Daddy's chicken coop looked much nicer than the old one. In fact, it looked a lot like the outdoor playhouse he had built for her that was in the small backyard of the condominium they used to live in back in the city. There was a wire fence in the front with a gate and the small building was made of plywood walls with a front door and two very small windows on each side and had a pitched roof.

Kaylee carried the basket in the crook of her arm and opened the gate. She stepped into the run and made sure to close the gate behind her.

There, Daddy! I did it!

She grabbed the knob and opened the door. As soon as the light shone in, the chickens started cackling and rustling their feathers. Kaylee spotted the white chickens right away sitting above their nest boxes.

Her father had made them a wonderful home.

Kaylee walked slowly up to the roost. One of the leghorns looked at her suspiciously and bobbed its head. Curious to see if the chicken had laid an egg, Kaylee reached out, trying her best not to scare the bird.

The hen squawked and pecked Kaylee's hand anyway.

"Ouch!" Maybe this wasn't going to be as easy as she thought. She extended her hand again. "I won't hurt you. I just...ouch." she yelped as another chicken on the ground came up and poked her shin with its sharp beak.

Kaylee backed up toward the open door.

She wondered if these were Josie's mean chickens and that's why she was so eager to give them away.

Kaylee looked sternly at the white chickens nestled on their perches.

The chickens stared back.

Something caught her eye and she looked down.

It was Bunny.

And on the ground under her feathery rump was a large blue egg.

"Oh my," Kaylee said. She squatted, picked up the egg, and placed it in her basket. "Thank you, Bunny."

The friendly chicken came over like it wanted Kaylee to pick it up, so she did. She glared at the rest of the brood. "Bad chickens!"

Kaylee stepped out of the coop but didn't close the door as she had Bunny in her arms and was carrying the basket. The other chickens seemed content to remain inside the coop, which was a little warmer than outside.

"Bunny, you want to play in the snow?" Kaylee put the bird down and it immediately started running on the cold ground, leaving little weird W-shaped impressions. Kaylee laughed and chased her pet chicken.

Bunny flapped her wings and flew over the fence.

"No, come back!" Kaylee watched in horror as Bunny trotted off.

Kaylee rushed to the gate then remembered she'd left the door to the coop open and if Bunny could fly, the others could too if they got out. She went back and closed the door. She dashed to the gate and opened it, making sure she closed it behind her and ran as fast as she could and followed Bunny's tiny tracks.

The chicken was heading in the direction of Josie's farm, which meant that the bird would have to cross the creek. Kaylee doubted if the bird could swim and knew if she didn't stop it in time it would drown for sure.

She was already in enough trouble even though it really wasn't her fault. She'd kept the gate closed just like her father had said, but he had never mentioned anything about chickens being able to fly.

Kaylee ran as fast as she could, but the snow was getting deeper as she went through the trees. She could hear the creek up ahead.

Oh, Bunny. Please don't drown.

She trudged through the snow and was almost to the water's edge when she suddenly stopped as a giant was blocking her path.

It was much taller than her father.

The creature looked a lot like Chewbacca, her favorite character in *Star Wars* though the hair all over its body was considerably shorter and it was much more muscular. It looked down at her with its large black eyes. Kaylee watched the steam coming out of its nostrils and the corner of its mouth.

She remembered a bedtime story Daddy would read her about a monster that lived in the woods and ate children, but then Mom told him to stop, as she didn't want Kaylee having nightmares.

Was this the monster from the woods?

That ate children?

No, this monster had a kind face.

"Hello," Kaylee said.

The giant stared down at her.

Kaylee reached inside her basket and took out the blue egg.

She held it up and offered it to the giant. "Here. Do you want it?"

The creature looked at the egg clutched in her tiny fingers.

Then extended its enormous hand.

Kaylee was about to place the egg in the black, leathery palm when she saw something dangling in the giant's other hand.

It was her pet chicken, Bunny.

27

After Marcus had washed up at the kitchen sink, he sat down at the table. Libby had made him a roast beef and Swiss cheese sandwich, which she'd put on a plate and placed on the table with a tall glass of well water. He'd been hungrier than he thought and quickly wolfed the sandwich down. He gulped the refreshing water and put the empty glass back down on the table. "That hit the spot."

"Glad you liked it," Libby said, standing at the counter with a dishrag in her hand.

Marcus got up from the table. He brought his dirty plate and glass over and put them in the sink half filled with warm, soapy water. He cleaned his plate, rinsed it off under the faucet, and handed the dish to Libby. She dried the plate and put it away in a cabinet then took the glass once Marcus had rinsed it. After drying the glass, she placed it in another cabinet next to a similar set of other glasses.

"I'm surprised Kaylee isn't back in by now," Marcus said. "When I brought the cages into the coop I noticed that a couple of the chickens had already laid eggs. I placed them in one of the nest boxes for her to find."

"Maybe she didn't see them," Libby said.

"I thought I left them in plain sight."

"We should go help her."

"Okay." Marcus went over and took his jacket off the back of his chair and put it on. He helped Libby with her coat. "Better put on your gloves, it's pretty chilly outside."

They stepped out of the house and went down the porch steps to the chicken coop.

"You did a nice job," Libby said, complimenting Marcus on his carpentry skills.

"Just something I threw together."

"Kaylee!" Libby called out.

Marcus expected Kaylee to yell back from inside the small building, but there was no reply. He was relieved to see the gate closed and the door to the coop was shut.

Good Girl. See, rules aren't so bad.

Marcus swung open the gate and stepped into the run. He waited until Libby came in then closed the gate. He went over, opened the door, and entered the coop.

"Kaylee, are you in here?" Libby asked, following Marcus inside.

Marcus looked around. The chickens were accounted for except for one. "Where's Bunny?"

"She's not in here?"

"No, I don't see her."

"You don't think Kaylee took her out?"

"She better not have. Not if she doesn't want it to run off." Marcus turned and strode out of the coop. He waited for Libby to come out then shut the door. He looked at the snow-covered ground and Kaylee's footprints leading to the coop and back to the gate. He also saw the chicken's imprints in the snow, going up the run then suddenly disappearing before reaching the fence.

"Look," Marcus said directing Libby's attention to Bunny's tracks that mysteriously seemed to end abruptly.

"What, don't tell me that chicken just got up and flew away," Libby said in a scoffing tone.

"That's exactly what it did."

"Marcus, chickens can't fly."

"For short distances they can. I guess Josie never clipped her wings."

"So you think Kaylee went after her?"

"Must have." Marcus opened the gate, stepped through, and shut it after Libby came out. He immediately scouted around and quickly found the chicken and Kaylee's tracks leading into the woods.

"Where do you think they're going?" Libby asked as she broke into a slow jog.

"Damn chicken must be part homing pigeon," Marcus said, keeping pace alongside Libby. "It's running back to Josie's."

"What if Kaylee gets lost?"

"Don't worry, we'll find her."

"Kaylee! It's Mom, where are you?" Libby yelled.

Marcus could hear the creek up ahead. He looked over at Libby and could tell she heard it too.

"Oh my God, Marcus. Is that water?"

"There's a creek up ahead."

"You know Kaylee can't swim."

Marcus charged through the shin-high snow, Libby stepping in his tracks to keep up. He could see the brook up ahead, channeling behind the trees.

Something was lying in the snow at the water's edge.

He leaned forward and trudged toward it.

"It's the basket you gave Kaylee," Libby gasped.

Marcus picked the empty basket up by the handle.

"Why would she just leave it?"

Possible scenarios played out in Marcus' head—none of them good.

He could see Kaylee's footprints on the snowy embankment heading upstream toward a fallen tree that stretched across the creek.

"Kaylee!" he yelled, his heart racing as he envisioned Kaylee attempting to cross and falling into the water. Unable to swim, sucked under and swept away, scared out of her mind, frantically fighting for her life as her lungs filled up and she drowned.

All while he sat at the kitchen table eating his lunch, without the least inclination that he would never see his daughter alive ever again.

Libby grabbed him by the arm. "I see her!"

Kaylee was standing in the snow at the end of the crude footbridge. She was holding Bunny in her arms.

Marcus and Libby hastened over to their daughter.

"Oh my God, Kaylee, you had us so worried," Libby said, kneeling in the snow and placing both her hands on the girl's shoulders, looking her up and down to make sure she wasn't injured in anyway.

"Here, let me take Bunny," Marcus said.

Kaylee handed the chicken over to Marcus and he tucked the bird firmly under his arm.

"Are you okay?" Libby asked unable to contain her tears of joy.

"Mom, why are you crying? Did I do something wrong?"

"No, you did nothing wrong," Marcus said. "We know what happened. Bunny flew the coop."

Libby glanced up, shook her head at him, and managed a smile.

"How'd you know?" Kaylee asked.

"Parents know things."

"I saw it."

"Saw what, Kaylee?"

"The monster from the book."

Marcus must have had a puzzled look on his face because Kaylee then said, "You know, the bedtime story. The monster that lives in the woods."

"Really, you saw a monster?"

"I did. And he caught Bunny for me."

"Is that right," Marcus said, skeptically.

"Honey, you're imagining things," Libby said.

"No, I'm not. He's real," Kaylee insisted.

"Oh, yeah?" Marcus said with a smirk. "If I recall correctly, he likes to eat children. So why didn't he eat you?"

"I don't know. Maybe he already ate."

28

Red was sitting on his ATV, having a drink when Boyd raced toward him in the trees. The rear tires of Boyd's quad fishtailed in the snow and he held onto the handlebars, steering against the turn to prevent the bike from flipping over. His boots and pant legs were covered in wet snow. He pulled up beside Red and turned off his engine.

"Any for me?" he asked Red, holding his hand out.

Red gave Boyd the near-empty Mason jar.

Boyd tilted back the glass container and drank the rest of the moonshine. He wiped his mouth with his sleeve and bent his arm back to heave the jar.

"No, you don't," Red said, blocking Boyd's throwing arm. "Less you want to fork over the deposit."

"Ah, sorry Red. I forgot." Boyd gave the jar back to Red, who screwed the lid back on, and stuffed the glass container inside a duffle bag strapped to the cargo bed on the back of his quad.

"See anything?" Red asked.

"Nothing."

They turned to the sound of an engine and saw Jesse on the opposite bank.

As soon as Jesse spotted Red and Boyd, he gunned his quad across the shallow creek. He stood up and held onto the handlebars as the ATV bounced over the rocky bottom and went airborne at one point, slamming down hard on the rough surface.

Jesse cleared the water, sped over, and kicked up a spray of snow as he skidded to a complete stop.

"Well?" Red said.

"I found some tracks then they stopped. They must have crossed over. I'd say they're heading for the river."

"Then they shouldn't be too hard to find," Red said.

"Any shine left?" Jesse asked.

"Nope," Red replied.

"Damn."

"Move out," Red said, firing up his quad.

Jesse started his engine and raced ahead.

Red and Boyd followed behind.

They hadn't traveled more than a mile when Jesse slowed down and stopped. He waited for Red and Boyd to pull up alongside.

"We got tracks," Jessie said, pointing at the footprints leading up the steep slope.

"That's them, all right," Boyd said. "Leading up to Kaine's cabin."

"We won't be able to get our quads up that," Jesse said after studying the terrain. "We're going to have to hike up."

"Then, that's what we'll do," Red said. "Grab your guns, boys. We're going to kill two birds with one stone."

"How's that, Red?" Boyd asked.

"After we get rid of those two we can stock up on more shine," Red said, lifting his duffle bag from the cargo bed, along with his short-barrel shotgun with the pistol grip.

29

Rhett Sawyer followed the narrow road through the dense forest and down through a gulch then stopped at the locked gate blocking the lane and turned off the engine. He grabbed some of the mail out of the bin on the passenger seat and sifted through the envelopes and magazines, selecting those that corresponded with the address on the mailbox attached to the fence post anchoring the hinges of the gate.

He got out of the Jeep and walked over to the mailbox. He opened the door and found there was still mail from the day before stuffed inside. He didn't know much about the people residing at this address, only that they were reclusive. There could have been a number of reasons why they hadn't bothered to retrieve their mail, and rather than stand around in the cold pondering what they might be, Rhett shoved today's mail into the box and closed the door.

He didn't care much for making the trip down to this spot because it was pretty much a dead end without much room to turn around. And now it was going to be especially tricky as there were rocks buried under the snow. If he wasn't careful he could snap the driveshaft or punch a hole in the oil pan.

The last thing he wanted was to get stranded out here in the middle of nowhere.

He couldn't call for help because he didn't have a radio in his mail truck and never carried one of those fancy cell phones, as everyone always complained they got poor or no reception up in the mountains.

Rhett climbed back inside behind the steering wheel and started up the truck.

He leaned out the open door and glanced back to make sure there was enough room for him to reverse and gave it some gas.

The tires crunched back over the snow.

He shifted into gear and pulled forward.

He stopped then backed up again.

Certain that he had enough room to maneuver the rest of the turn, Rhett put the transmission into gear and put his foot down on the accelerator.

Only the truck wouldn't move as the rear tires were spinning.

So he pressed down harder on the pedal.

The truck lurched forward. Rhett fought to regain control of the steering wheel as it spun out of his hands and he was thrown into the mail bin on the passenger seat.

His foot came off of the gas pedal, but not before the vehicle took a hard bounce and crashed down in the snow.

A little shaken, Rhett scooted off the driver's seat and slid down onto the snowy ground.

He could hear a hissing sound. He walked around to the other side of the mail truck and saw the back tire slowly deflating.

"Damn my luck," Rhett swore. He knew he was too old to set out trudging through the snow and looking for help. It would be suicide in this blustering weather. The closest people were the ones he had just delivered to, and seeing as they hadn't collected yesterday's mail, he doubted if anyone was even around.

It had been a while since he had changed a tire, but what choice did he have.

Rhett stepped to the back of the truck and raised the rollup door. He pushed a couple of mail bins out of the way and lifted the cover on the recessed compartment that housed the spare tire, jack, and lug wrench.

He was relieved to find the tire fully inflated and had not lost pressure sitting around for so long. He struggled lifting the tire out and dropped it in the snow.

Grabbing the lug wrench, Rhett started loosening the lug nuts. He went around the outside of the rim and removed all but one so that the flat tire wouldn't fall off while he was jacking up the truck.

He took the jack and placed it under the chassis. He inserted the beveled end of the tire iron into the slot and began pumping the handle. Slowly, that side of the truck began to rise. When it was high enough and the bottom of the tire was off the ground, Rhett stopped, removed the last lug nut, and pulled off the flat tire.

He was reaching for the spare when he heard something behind him in the trees.

Accompanied by a low menacing growl.

Rhett slowly turned his head to look over his shoulder.

All he saw was a black face and sharp fangs coming straight for him.

Rhett dove and scrambled under the truck. His shoulder slammed into the jack and the undercarriage of the truck came crashing down...

Right on top of Rhett.

The mailman yelled and screamed in agonizing pain, the side of his face pressed to the ground. He peered out from under the truck and saw ribbons of blood, spurting out onto the snow.

Jesus, Rhett. If only you hadn't been so stubborn and just retired. None of this would be happening.

And that ravenous beast wouldn't be hunched in the snow, devouring your leg.

30

Cole used the process of elimination and began separating the gun parts on the table in different groups so that he could narrow it down and reassemble at least one of the firearms. There was an oily rag and a can of gun cleaning fluid with a squirt applicator next to a box of nine-millimeter ammunition. A dozen bullets were standing on end with carved Xs on the tips made by a very sharp knife.

"This guy's been making his own hollow points."

"What are those?" Kate asked. She tore down the black plastic and stared out the window.

"There're nasty bullets, made to do serious damage."

"Do you have any idea what you're doing?" Kate asked.

"Have a little faith," he replied.

Cole picked up a molded handgrip with the lower slide portion of a semi-automatic and knew it was for a Hi Power Browning as it had an engraving on the gunmetal blue finish. He matched up a barrel, but was having difficulty figuring what kept the piece attached to the bottom slide portion. Then he saw the tiny hook and figured there must be a spring. There were two springs on the table. He chose a spring and slipped one end inside the slide, but the metal coil was kinked and wouldn't extend properly. He took it out, flipped it over, and it fit perfectly.

Cole took the barrel section and slipped it back over the lower slide. He figured there must be a part that would lock the two pieces together; and there was, a rocker arm-looking slide lock and release that snapped into place.

He tested the gun and slid back the action a couple times to make sure it worked correctly. "Well, what do you think?" Cole said and held up the gun to show off his handiwork.

"I think you better hurry up," Kate answered.

"Why, what is it?"

Kate turned away from the window and stared at Cole. "It's them. They found us!"

***

Avery drove down to Kaine Brown's cabin.

It was high time he paid the man another visit.

Check up on that dog.

He thought he would hassle Kaine, demand to see a business license for selling alcohol—even though he knew damn well the man didn't have one—or at the minimum, cite him for animal cruelty. Put a little scare into him or at least try. Kaine wasn't one to scare easily, especially when the moonshiner was brave enough to sell his whiskey and share company with the most unsavory and dangerous men living on the mountain.

As soon as he pulled the Bronco into the small clearing, he knew something wasn't right. A door to the equipment shed had been left open. Avery could see the boiler inside and lots of broken glass strewn on the dirt.

Avery glanced through the windshield and looked for the dog, but he didn't see it anywhere. Maybe it was frozen to death under that crate.

But then he saw something black, half buried in the snow.

His immediate reaction was that Kaine had set the dog on fire and watched with pleasure, as the poor thing died an excruciating death.

"Kaine, you bastard," Avery cursed. At least now, he had something to arrest Kaine for.

It was time to put Kaine out of business, once and for all.

The court would swoop in and seize Kaine's assets while Avery held the bootlegger for arraignment in his jail cell. Hopefully the prosecutor would be from a generation of prohibitionists—as well as being an animal lover—and would expose Kaine for the heinous person he truly was and get a stiff conviction, sentencing him to a long stint in the upstate penitentiary.

Avery reached over, grabbed his Stetson off the passenger seat, and opened the driver door. He stepped out onto the snow and squared his hat on his head.

He saw three men appear from the side of the shed.

It was Red and two of his men, Boyd and Jesse. He noticed they were carrying guns.

As soon as Red saw Avery standing behind the open truck door, he stopped in his tracks, as did Boyd and Jesse.

Avery glanced over their shoulders expecting to see Seth, but the man wasn't with them.

"Sheriff," Red said.

Still standing behind the open door, Avery replied, "Red. I'm afraid you boys made a wasted trip. I'm here to arrest Kaine."

"That so," Red said. He looked at Boyd then Jesse. The two men nodded and took a couple steps away from Red and spread out.

Avery used the concealment of the door and slowly reached down for his gun. It was cold enough that his breath was fogging up the window glass.

"I don't want any trouble," Avery said.

"Neither do we," Red said.

Avery heard a muffled cry. He looked over at the cabin and saw a woman inside, banging on the window.

Then out of the corner of his eye, Avery saw Red come up with his scattergun and fire.

The side window shattered, blasting shards into Avery's face, the deadly pellets riddling the metal door, heavy buckshot tearing into his knees and shins, buckling his legs.

His boots scooted out from under him and he slid down onto his butt, his gun half drawn out of the holster.

"Finish him," Red said to Jesse.

Avery could hear footsteps crunching in the snow. He drew his gun all the way out of the holster, and with only the approaching sound to guide him, Avery pointed the muzzle of his revolver under the bottom of the door, aimed upward, and fired.

The crunching continued, one step then another.

Jesse came into view and stood five feet away, staring directly at Avery. The gun in Jesse's hand slipped from his fingers and dropped into the snow.

He clamped his hand over the smoldering hole in his throat. Blood squirted out between his fingers. Jesse dropped to his knees. He gurgled up a mouthful of blood and fell facedown in the snow.

Avery leaned out so he could see around the lip of the door.

Boyd was running toward the cabin.

Avery saw Red pointing his shotgun at him and ducked back just as the man fired.

The driver door was peppered, but none of the pellets struck Avery.

Avery shoved his gun barrel under the driver door and fired off a wild shot hoping he might get lucky and take down Boyd.

Another shot rang out.

Avery felt the bullet punch into his side. The pain was fierce. His gun fell out of his hand and he slowly slumped over in the snow.

He could see Boyd kicking in the front door and firing two shots into the cabin.

A series of bright flashes appeared from inside the gloomy cabin accompanied by roaring gunshots.

Boyd jerked and staggered back; each bullet slamming into his chest, blood spurting as it exited out his back. He fell onto the snow with his arms spread wide apart like he was about to make a snow angel.

The cabin door slammed shut.

Avery looked down at the blood under him and felt suddenly drowsy.

So he closed his eyes and drifted off.

31

Weston Egger stood on the runners of his Ski Doo, jumped a snow bank, and went airborne for ten feet. He bent his knees as the machine touched down and his butt landed on the padded seat. The snowmobile kicked up a white plume as he headed farther up into the trees.

Normally, he wouldn't be this far up the mountain at this hour as it meant having to return home in the dark. But Weston had promised Avery he would check his trap line and he was a man of his word. He wasn't worried being out by himself. He'd hiked and hunted most of this side of the mountain and knew the landscape like a mapmaker knew his topography.

Weston had prepared for a cold evening. He wore a trapper-style hat with earflaps, waterproof gloves, a heavy parka, snow pants, and fur-lined boots.

His hunting rifle was strapped across his back on a sling.

He stopped the snowmobile near a cluster of boulders and turned off the engine.

From here, he would have to set out on foot.

Weston dismounted and grabbed a pair of snowshoes off the cargo bed. He placed the footwear on the ground, which looked like two fish-shaped tennis rackets without the handles. He stepped on the snowshoes and strapped them to his boots.

He grabbed the sling and slipped his rifle off his back. He slid the bolt back, put a round in the chamber, and thumbed on the safety. He made sure to pop off the lens covers on the high power scope just in case he saw some game and needed to get off a quick shot.

Leaning the rifle against the side of the snowmobile, Weston grabbed a small rucksack that had a bota bag of drinking water, some granola bars, and an emergency survival kit and slipped one strap over his shoulder.

Weston slung his rifle over the other shoulder.

Using two ski poles, he started up the slope. The poles were necessary for ensuring the ground was safe to walk on before taking a step and enabled him to keep his balance in the deep snow.

Even though no one had anticipated the early winter storm, Weston had marked each location where he had set up a trap with an orange six-foot tall pole. The traps would be easy to find buried under the snow. He certainly didn't want to be traipsing through knee-high snow and step in one of his own traps, especially being out all by himself and with no one around to help him.

After a ten-minute hike, he came to the first orange marker.

He used a ski pole and cleared away some of the snow. He could tell that the snare hadn't been tripped and carefully covered it back up.

He continued on to the next pole. After careful inspection, he found the trap hadn't been sprung, and went on to the next one.

Weston came to a snow-covered log. He stood on the log with both snowshoes and placed the tips of his ski poles on the other side. Making sure the ground was solid ahead of him, Weston stepped down in the snow.

He could see the orange pole up ahead. He'd tied a green ribbon around the shaft, indicating there was a forty-pound bear trap buried under the snow, powerful enough to snap a 2 x 4 inch board completely in half.

Weston had used the trap to bag various predators that threatened the mountain community. He remembered the time he caught a one hundred fifty pound mountain lion that had been terrorizing sheep farmers and how it laid its claws into him before he was able to shoot it.

Another time he'd tangled with a seven-foot grizzly stuck in the same trap. The powerful bear had pulled the stake holding down the trap completely out of the ground and charged Weston, who had to fight it with only a hunting knife. Luckily, the animal had lost a lot of blood, and Weston was able to slay the bear even though he had been savagely mauled, later spending a month in the hospital recuperating from his wounds.

He stopped ten feet short of reaching the marker.

Something big was lying by the base of the pole.

Weston sidestepped in his snowshoes and circled the thing so he could study it from every angle.

He'd never seen anything like it.

One thing was for sure; this certainly wasn't a Bigfoot.

Judging by its size, Weston guesstimated that it had to weigh at least three hundred pounds. It was lying on its right side. The right rear leg was stretched out, half buried in the snow, its foot no doubt imprisoned in the deadly jaws of the bear trap as the snow was saturated with rust-colored blood.

If he had to categorize the animal, he would have to place it in the canine family, but nothing like a wolf. This animal had short brown hair on a taut hide. Its upper body was enormous like a wild boar and had bull-like muscular shoulders and biceps. A dark brown longhair ridgeback mane ran from its forehead down to the middle of its spine.

The hindquarters were brawny and it had a brown twelve-inch long dog-like tail.

Weston gazed down at the left leg. Like the rest of the animal, the limb was sinewy and well defined. Sharp claws protruded from the four-knuckle paw. He could only imagine the serious damage they could do to a prey. The talons were hooked making him wonder if the animal could scale trees.

The head was huge, mostly a blackish-brown with small rounded ears on the crown of its skull. Its left eye was closed, but its mouth was open. Weston could see six upper teeth between two long fangs. The lower jaw had eight incisors in the front then a gap in the gum line and another row of bone-crushing molars stretching back into its savage mouth.

Being an outdoorsman he thought he was familiar with every animal in the region. Living on the mountain he'd heard just about every legend and Native American Indian myth about forest creatures, but nothing resembling this.

Could it be a descendant of the dire wolf?

But they'd been extinct for tens of thousands of years.

No, this was definitely a crossbreed between two separate species, but he had no idea what they could be. There was no telling what went on in the remotest regions deep in the forest.

Maybe some wild beast had hopped a fence and mated with a large domestic animal. Anything was possible.

And where had it come from? Had it been hidden all these years and suddenly migrated to this side of the mountain searching for food having depleted its own resources?

So now Weston had proof that it wasn't a Bigfoot that had been killing Lou Cobb's sheep.

It had been this predator.

Not that either one seemed believable. He'd thought Avery was losing his mind when he told him he'd found a Bigfoot imprint in the snow. Weston wondered what he'd think once he saw this strange beast.

He figured it would be easier to transport the carcass down the mountain than to get Avery to hike up.

But first he would have to pry open the jaws on the bear trap and release the animal's leg.

Then it would be a matter of dragging the body over to a good spot where he could roll it down the hill. From there, he could hitch it to the back of his snowmobile and tow it back to his lodge.

Weston removed the rucksack strap from his shoulder and let the canvas bag drop to the ground. He slipped the sling off his other shoulder and stood his rifle up against a tree trunk.

He went over, unsnapped his snowshoes, and got down on his knees. The snow was cold through the waterproof fabric of his ski pants. He reached down with one glove and began scooping up big handfuls of snow. He kept digging until he saw the metal bridge and the steel teeth closed tight around the animal's lower leg. It was difficult to determine the extent of the injury by just looking at it, but Weston wouldn't be surprised if the bone hadn't been pulverized by the powerful spring action.

Lying in the hole was a two-foot long steel rod, which Weston always left beneath the trap so that he could use it as a pry bar to open the high-tension trap.

After years of experience, he had little trouble wedging the end of the rod between the meshed teeth and opened them up. He used the bottom of his boot to hold the jaws apart and was able to lift the leg out before the trap snapped shut.

Weston stood and took a step back.

That's when he saw the animal's chest heave.

The left eye opened and looked directly at Weston.

All this time, he'd thought the damn thing was dead, but it was only playing possum. Waiting for him to release it from the trap.

Which meant it was not only cunning, but possessed a high degree of intelligence.

Weston backed toward the tree where he had left his rifle.

The creature never took its eyes off Weston as it pushed itself up off the snow.

Standing on all fours, but favoring its injured right hind leg, it looked especially menacing. It hunched its massive shoulders and snarled at Weston.

He knew even with the lame leg the monstrous creature could leap the short distance before he could dive for his gun.

For some strange reason, the animal didn't seem anxious to make the first move, but instead watched Weston like it was biding its time and didn't feel the least bit threatened.

Weston heard heavy breathing like horse-like snorts. He slowly turned his head and looked over his shoulder.

Three similar creatures as the one before him were standing shoulder to shoulder, staring at him. Thick drool hung from their mouths; white fangs glistening as they bared their vicious teeth.

For some reason he'd thought this was a solitary predator.

He hadn't considered there was more than one and that they ran in a pack.

Weston lunged for his gun.

The unmerciful pack was swift and pounced on him before he could take a second step. Crushing him to the ground, the ferocious creatures ripped the hunter apart with their savage teeth like a pride of lions tearing into a fresh kill.

32

Cole lay on the floor, bleeding. It was nighttime outside and pitch black inside the cabin. He could hear Kate moving towards him.

"Stay down," he warned.

"How bad is it?"

"He got me in the shoulder." Cole had just slapped the magazine clip with the hollow point bullets up inside the Browning's handgrip and cocked back the slide when Boyd kicked in the front door and fired two shots, one of the bullets striking Cole in the left shoulder.

The impact had almost sent him flying backwards, but his knees had banged up against the bottom of the table and kept him from tipping over. He already had his right arm fully extended, aiming at the front door, so it was just a matter of pulling the trigger as many times as he could before he gave into the pain and fell out of the chair onto the floor.

Boyd had been a big man, but the hollow points had packed quite a wallop and cut him down to size.

Cole had never pointed a gun at another human being before, let alone killed a person. He probably would have felt some degree of remorse if the man hadn't been out to kill him and his shoulder didn't feel like a blacksmith had stabbed him with a hot poker.

He could hear Kate rummaging through what sounded like her backpack then a small light came on, illuminating the floor area.

"Is that your headlamp?"

"That's right."

"Whatever you do, don't put it on, and don't stand up. You'll be a sitting duck if they see you through the window."

Kate stayed low and scooted across the floor. She placed the LED light next to Cole so she could examine his shoulder. "I need you to get out of your coat so I can check your wound."

"Easier said than done," Cole grimaced.

"No whining, just do it."

Cole rolled to one side. Kate held onto the cuff while Cole pulled his arm out of the sleeve.

Kate tore part of his shirt and examined the gunshot wound. "You're lucky, the bullet went all the way through." She'd taken a shirt from her backpack and used it as a compress to staunch the bleeding. "Take your hand and put pressure on it."

"Sure thing, Nurse Jackie." Cole held the garment against his shoulder.

"Does it hurt?"

"Duh. Where's the gun?"

Kate looked around the floor. "Right here." She picked the pistol up by the handgrip and placed it next to Cole.

"Any idea what's going on outside?"

"Let me go see."

"Careful. Don't make yourself a target."

Cole watched as Kate crept across the floor to the wall. She rose slowly and peeked out the window.

"I can see the sheriff lying by his truck. His door's open so the interior light is on."

"Is he dead?" Cole asked.

"I don't know. He's not moving."

"What about the others?"

"The one you shot is laying in the snow. He's dead for sure. There's another one by the truck. The sheriff must have shot him."

"Where's the old man? Red?"

Kate ducked under the windowsill, moved to the other side of the glass, and peered out. "He's built a fire and is sitting in the doorway of the shed with a blanket around his shoulders and his shotgun across his lap."

"Is he looking this way?"

"Oh yeah. And he's drinking a jar of moonshine."

"Good. Maybe he'll get drunk and pass out."

"Why does he just sit out there?" Kate asked. "How come he hasn't tried to bust in?"

"I bet he's been here before and knows there's no backdoor to this place. He's going to wait us out. Shoot us the second we step out the door."

"Sooner or later, he's going to fall asleep," Kate said. "Especially out there in the cold. If only we could...oh, my God."

"What is it?"

"The sheriff. He just moved."

"You mean he's alive?" Cole scooted across the floor and sat up with his back against the wall.

"We have to do something," Kate said. "We can't just leave him out there to freeze to death."

"You said you could see inside his truck?"

"Yes, the dome light's on."

"He must have a two-way radio."

Kate crouched and looked at Cole. "What do you think? We wait for Red to fall asleep and I sneak out? Call for help?"

"That's the plan. Let's hope the old man isn't an insomniac."

33

Arlene bent over and opened the oven door. She reached in with her mitts, grabbed both handles, and took out the roasting pan. She kicked the door closed with the heel of her shoe and placed the pan on the drain board to cool.

An annoying moth kept flying repeatedly into the glass light bulb over the kitchen table making a *dinking* sound. She tried to catch it, but the bug stayed close to the ceiling and was always just out of reach.

Lou came down the stairs after washing up and entered the kitchen. He gave Arlene a big smile. "Do I smell pot roast?"

"With red potatoes and carrots."

"I'll bring down the plates." Lou went over and opened a cabinet door. He took out two dinner plates then paused. "Are we having dessert?"

"Cobbler and custard."

Lou grabbed two small dessert plates as well and closed the door. He placed the plates on the table. He opened a drawer and gathered their cutlery. Napkins were in a dispenser on the table along with a peppershaker, but no salt as the doctor had told Lou to cut down on his sodium intake.

Lou arranged the table.

"Shall we have wine with dinner?" Arlene asked.

"Yes, I could go for a little vino." Lou opened the pantry door. He brought out a one-gallon glass jug of red wine and put it on the counter. He poured the beverage into two wineglasses and brought them to the table, sipping on his glass as he had filled it to the brim and didn't want to spill a drop on Arlene's nice clean floor.

Arlene went over to the sink to rinse off a serving spoon.

Lou ambled over. "Anything else I can do?"

"I think that's it. Have you heard anything back from Avery?"

"Nope, not a word."

A motion-activated floodlight turned on outside and they both looked out the kitchen window.

"It's out there again," Lou said.

"What is?"

"The Bigfoot."

"Lou, don't be absurd."

"Arlene, I saw the footprint."

The light turned off on the short timer and everything went dark.

Lou and Arlene could hear the sheep bleating.

"They sound scared, Lou."

"You stay here. I'll go check on them."

"I'm coming with you." Arlene undid her apron and threw it on a chair.

"No." Lou stormed into the mudroom. He grabbed his coat off the hook and snatched up his double-barrel shotgun. He opened the breech to make sure it was loaded then snapped the gun closed.

"You're going to need me to hold the flashlight," Arlene said, ignoring her husband's plea for her to stay inside the house, and putting on her jacket.

"It's too dangerous out there."

"So?"

"Is there no talking to you?"

"Quit with the macho baloney and let's go."

Lou nudged open the screen door and they went outside.

"My God it's cold," Arlene said, shivering as she turned on the flashlight.

"See, you should have stayed inside."

"Just go buster." Arlene shone the beam on the ground and they slowly approached the pens. The sheep were restless, pressing their bodies close to one another, not for warmth, but out of fear.

Lou stopped and faced the woods. He tried listening for anything that might be out there, but the sheep were making too much noise. It wasn't like he could yell for them to shut up.

Arlene panned the beam of her flashlight at the edge of the trees.

They saw nothing, but foliage.

"Switch off your light," Lou said.

Arlene didn't question and turned off the flashlight.

It felt eerie standing in the pitch black. Lou had hoped his senses would be more attuned without the light, but it was impossible to concentrate with all the commotion the sheep were making.

Three of the six floodlights came on at the same time: a single light at each end and one near the middle.

"That's impossible," Lou said, "How could...?" and then it dawned on him. For three lights to get triggered at the exact same time there had to be three of them.

Lou and Arlene watched in horror as a massive creature appeared from the gloom and stepped under the bright floodlight centered between the other two security lights.

"Oh my God, Lou. Is that a mountain lion?"

"I don' think so," he replied as this animal was three times the size of any cougar he had ever seen. It looked like a razorback hog, but moved like a big cat on the prowl.

Arlene grabbed Lou's arm. "Let's go back to the house."

Another creature appeared at the far end and stood in the light, shoulders hunched, a stiff mane running halfway down its back.

Lou glanced at the other spotlight nearest the house. A third beast was standing in the ring of light. Its head was down, taking the posture of a stalking wolf even though it looked more like a young bull without horns from this distance.

"Once they move away from those trees, those lights are going to turn off. When they do, run like hell," Lou said.

"You honestly think we can outrun them?"

"We'll have to try. Switch off the flashlight." He figured it was thirty yards back to the house. They had the light in the kitchen window to guide them.

Arlene turned off the light.

Lou watched the creatures slowly advance.

The three floodlights switched off simultaneously.

"Run!" Lou grabbed Arlene by the arm and they dashed for the house. He could hear heavy footfalls behind him, but they weren't coming after them; the damn things were going for the sheep. He was tempted to stop and go back to protect his livestock, which would have meant leaving Arlene and that wouldn't do.

Besides, there was another one of those creatures lurking just out of reach of the floodlight near the house.

Another floodlight came on—different from the others.

Lou glanced to his left and saw an additional creature stride out of the trees.

Goddamn, there're four of them?

"Hurry, hurry," Lou shouted when they reached the side of the house. He flung open the screen door and pushed Arlene inside. Turning around, he saw one of the creatures bolting toward him. He raised his shotgun and fired off one barrel. The buckshot pelted the animal's back, causing it to falter and almost go down before it veered out of the path of another possible shot and disappeared into the dark.

Lou followed Arlene into the kitchen.

He shut the door and locked it. Even though it was an exterior door and was fairly solid, it did have a glass window and was easily penetrable.

Arlene rushed to the phone hanging on the kitchen wall. She took the receiver off the cradle and started punching in the numbers.

There was a loud thump on the other side of the kitchen door. The glass pane shattered and the wood split down the middle.

"Forget the phone!" Lou yelled. "Get upstairs!"

Arlene dropped the receiver and ran for the stairwell.

Lou was right behind her as they hurried up to the landing.

He turned and pointed the shotgun just as one of the creatures barged into the kitchen, knocking over chairs and the table, dumping the plates on the floor, and sending glasses shattering, spilling red wine all over.

The monstrous head swiveled side-to-side, nostrils flared, picking up the scent.

Panting hard like a thoroughbred after a race, the stocky beast raised its head and gazed up at Lou. It edged slowly toward the bottom of the stairs. Lou noticed that the animal had a slight limp. He could see blood on its right rear leg where it must have injured itself.

Arlene had moved to their bedroom and was standing in the doorway. "Lou, get in here."

"But I still have one shell left."

"Don't be a fool. Get in here, now!"

Lou knew she was right. It would be foolhardy trying to fend off this creature with only one cartridge. He had more shells in the gun locker in the mudroom and his hunting rifle was locked up in the gun cabinet in the living room—a lot of good they were doing him downstairs.

He couldn't afford to waste the only shot he had, so he stepped back into the bedroom, and closed the door.

"Help me move the armoire." Lou stood on the side of the tall dresser and began pushing it across the hardwood floor. Arlene helped guide the piece of furniture so they could barricade the door.

Lou went over to the bedroom window.

A floodlight had triggered. Lou could see the pens. Some of the railings were knocked off their posts. The sheep were getting out, scattering across the yard, some into the trees, others running off into the night.

One of the powerful creatures had one of Lou's prize ewes down on the snowy ground. It burrowed its head into the sheep's belly and ripped it open with its sharp teeth.

The predator snapped back its head, tossing bloody entrails into the air.

"Son of a bitch!" Lou slammed the wall with the ball of his fist.

He counted at least 20 dead sheep.

Some had been partially eaten, but the others looked as if they had been killed merely for sport. He saw two of the creatures take off into the trees. He glanced about the yard, but didn't see the other one. He prayed they had their fill of blood and wouldn't chase down and slaughter the rest of his flock.

He heard heavy pounding beyond the bedroom door.

"Oh my God, Lou. There's one coming up the stairs."

"Get back." Lou stood in the middle of the room.

"What if it breaks in?" Arlene asked nervously, standing behind the bed.

"Let it try." Lou aimed his shotgun at the armoire in front of the door.

It was up on the landing, pacing the hall.

Lou could hear its throaty bellow, like a bull issuing a warning.

The floor planks groaned just outside the door.

And then a loud bang shook the room.

The armoire tipped into the room and smashed down on the floor.

A huge head poked through the split-open bedroom door. The monstrous creature parted the wood with its muscular shoulders and stepped up on the back panel of the armoire.

Lou pointed the muzzle of his shotgun and pulled the trigger.

The hammer came down, but nothing happened.

The shell was a dud.

"No, no," Lou said, and backed up. He looked at Arlene. "Love you."

Arlene gave him a weak smile—and the creature lunged.

The beast slammed down on its chest and clawed at the end of the pressboard backing of the dresser, but couldn't hold on, struggling as it was dragged back through the ruined door.

Lou rushed over, held Arlene, and they ducked down behind the bed.

They could hear a turbulent clash outside the door, brawny bodies banging against the walls. Pounding fists, snarling and snapping teeth.

A booming roar then a distressing yelp—a bone-crushing snap.

Followed by a thunderous crash and something landing on the ground floor with a heavy thud.

Arlene gave Lou a shocked look. "What in God's name was that?"

"I don't know. But whatever it was, it just saved our lives." Lou went over and peered out through the damaged door. He couldn't see anything on the landing. The stair banister was gone, smashed to smithereens.

Lou shoved the armoire out of the way. He grabbed what was left of the door and it broke off the hinges and fell onto the floor. He looked back at Arlene. "Stay here while I go look."

"Shut up, Lou. I'm coming with you."

"Fine."

He still had the shotgun in his hand even though it wasn't loaded. He figured he better keep it and reload once he was downstairs.

Lou went out onto the landing and looked down. The kitchen was destroyed.

Arlene gazed down. "My Lord, what a mess."

A wide red stain was on the floor and trailed through the demolished furniture and broken housewares out the door and into the mudroom.

Lou went down the stairs, Arlene right behind him. When they reached the bottom, Lou entered the kitchen and tried not to step in the blood. He poked his head in the doorway and looked inside the mudroom. The screen door was hanging wide open.

He bent down and retrieved some cartridges from the gun locker and loaded the shotgun. He glanced over at Arlene and saw that she had her flashlight ready.

"Careful," he said and stepped outside.

Arlene turned on the flashlight.

There was a long trail of blood leading into the trees.

"It dragged that thing away."

"What do you think it was?" Arlene asked.

"Look for yourself."

Arlene shined the beam on the large footprints in the snow just left of the crimson drag marks. "Lou, I don't believe it."

"Told you it was a Bigfoot."

34

Kate stayed by the window so she could keep watch on Red as he sat by his fire just outside the shed doorway. He hadn't bothered to add any more wood so the flames had diminished to glowing embers.

An empty canning jar was lying beside his chair.

She watched him slump forward, the blanket draped over his shoulders. The shotgun slipped off his lap and landed in the snow.

"About time he passed out," Kate said.

Cole moved across the cabin and crouched beside Kate.

"How's the shoulder?" she asked.

"Hurts like hell. I can barely move my arm."

"I'm going out there," Kate said.

"What if it's a trick?"

"I watched him polish off the whole jar."

"You should take the gun," Cole said and held out the Browning semi-automatic.

"No, you keep it."

"Are you sure?"

"You're better with it than I am."

"Okay. I can cover you."

"You better." Kate turned and faced Cole. "Kiss for luck."

Cole hugged her and gave her a big kiss. "Be careful."

Kate opened the door of the cabin just wide enough so she could slip through and still a gush of cold air blew in. She stayed low and crept out. Cole kept the door open a crack so he could keep watch over her.

Trying not to make her presence known, Kate stepped gingerly across the snow to the passenger side of the Bronco. She grabbed the door handle, disengaged the latch, and was relieved to find the door unlocked. As the dome light was already on as the driver door was ajar, she didn't have the worry of a sudden illumination giving her away.

She gazed through the frosty windshield. She could see the smoldering fire and Red's dark silhouette in the chair.

Kate got inside and kept her head down. She leaned over, an elbow on the center console between the bucket seats.

The two-way radio was mounted under the dashboard.

She grabbed the mike and switched on the radio. A loud screech came out of the speaker.

"Shit," she cursed under her breath. She quickly turned down the squelch knob and the noise stopped.

"Kate!" It was Cole.

Sitting up straight, Kate looked over at the cabin. Cole was waving his arm.

She turned and glanced out the windshield.

The chair by the shed was empty except for the blanket.

"Jesus," Kate said. She used the mike in her hand, smashed the dome light over her head, and the interior of the truck went dark.

She kept still and listened for footsteps.

Nothing.

Kate felt the mike in her hand. She'd cracked the casing by breaking the overhead light, rendering it useless. Maybe this hadn't been a good idea. She stretched across the driver seat to see if the sheriff was conscious. "Are you awake?" she whispered. "Can you hear me?"

The sheriff didn't respond.

"Yes, I hear you."

Kate spun around. Red grabbed her by the boot and yanked her out of the truck onto the snow. He grabbed her roughly by the arm and hoisted her up onto her feet.

"Get your damn hands off me," Kate protested.

"Shut up," he snapped and cuffed her alongside the head.

The blow sent her reeling, but he kept her on her feet. He shoved her around the back of the Bronco so Cole in the cabin couldn't see them.

"In the shed," Red ordered.

Kate stumbled in the snow. She was looking at the small fire Red had built when the tip of her boot snagged on something buried in the snow and she fell.

She screamed when she saw the grotesque human carcass of charred flesh and exposed raw meat.

"Well if it ain't Kaine Brown," Red said.

Kate heard a growl and turned.

A dark shape was slinking out of the crate ten feet away.

Red heard it too and faced the dog.

He held up his shotgun with one hand and pointed the barrel.

Gunshots rang out.

Kate turned and saw Cole hobbling in the snow, pointing his pistol, and firing at Red. She could tell he was in a lot of pain and wasn't aiming straight as the bullets kept missing, and were striking the side of the shed instead of Red.

Red swung the gun barrel toward Cole.

"Get down!" Kate yelled.

Cole dove onto the snow just as Red pulled the trigger. While Cole lay flat on the snow, Red pumped another round into the chamber.

The dog bolted across the snow.

Red trained his gun on the canine.

"No, you don't," the sheriff said, and shot Red twice.

The old man dropped his gun and toppled over in the snow.

The dog stopped short of the dead man and sat down.

Kate got to her feet.

Cole was struggling to get to his.

They went over to the Bronco.

"Thanks," Kate said, kneeling next to the wounded sheriff.

"Any of you know how to handle a four-wheel drive?" he asked.

"I do," Cole said, "but I doubt I can with this shoulder."

"I can get us out of here," Kate said.

"The road's pretty tricky," the sheriff said.

"Unless you'd rather we sat and froze to death?"

"Sorry, no offense." The sheriff managed a smile. "Keys are in the ignition."

"Good. Now let's get you two to a hospital," Kate said.

"Do me a favor," the sheriff said.

"What's that?" Kate asked.

"Bring the dog."

35

After her morning shower, Josie got dressed, and went out to the kitchen to make breakfast. Duke ambled in and headed straight for his food dish.

"What, can't I even have my coffee?"

Duke stared at the empty bowl. Josie knew his rationale—if he stared long enough, his chow would magically appear.

Which it always did, thanks to her.

She picked up his twenty-pound bag of dog food by the counter and filled his bowl. Then she made sure he had plenty of water.

Duke dove in greedily and gobbled up every nugget, even licking the dish, and covering it with white slobber. He lapped up his water and drank thirstily, splashing the hardwood floor.

Josie wiped up the puddle. She picked up his empty bowl and put it in the sink to be washed.

She peered out the window. There was more snow on the ground and tracks outside the livestock pen. Her first thought was coyotes had come around in the night for the goats. If the would-be predators were still lurking about, Duke would quickly chase them off.

Josie never knew Duke's true lineage as Lewis had found him as a pup wandering in the woods. They believed someone that no longer wanted the responsibility of dog ownership had abandoned him.

Lewis had given their newfound pet the name Duke, as he was a big fan of the actor John Wayne who played in the westerns. When Duke grew to be so big, Josie suspected he might have a strain of Rottweiler mixed in as he was a great guard dog.

Jose grabbed her coat from the peg on the wall and put it on.

She went over to the backdoor where she kept Lewis' single-shell shotgun leaning up against the wall. She always left the breech open and the cartridges up on top of the refrigerator. She reached up and snatched three shells. She popped one in the tube, closed the breech, and pocketed the other two.

Duke was watching her, his tail wagging with anticipation.

"Okay, go out and earn your room and board."

The big dog barked.

Josie opened the door and Duke bounded out.

He hadn't rounded the corner of the house when he started barking fiercely.

Racing out the door, Josie ran out into the yard. Duke was standing up on the wood railing, making a ruckus.

"What is it, boy?" Josie said, reaching the pen.

She looked inside and saw over a dozen goats lying on their sides in the snow.

Duke jumped down and ran around the side of the corral. He entered the enclosure through an opening where the fencing had been knocked down.

Josie opened the gate and rushed in to examine the goats.

Three of them had been mauled and were definitely dead.

She waited for a moment.

Slowly, one by one, the feigning goats jerked up and hopped to their feet.

"Thank God," Josie said.

She gazed about, expecting to see something lurking in the nearby trees, but saw nothing suspicious. She looked down and saw massive paw prints in the snow. They were too big to be a coyote.

Josie compared the prints with Duke's as he circled around the slain goats in a protective pattern even though they were dead.

The paw prints were more than twice the size of Duke's, which meant that whatever animal had killed her livestock, it had to be enormous.

Duke spun around and faced Josie. He snarled at her, startling Josie as he looked as if he was about to attack.

Josie looked down at the snow between her and Duke and saw a huge shadow loom over them. A heavy body slammed into her and sent her sprawling onto the ground, but she managed to hold onto the shotgun.

The panic-stricken goats bleated, some paralyzed and falling down, the others scattering and charging out through the open gate.

Josie turned her head and saw a monstrous creature standing in the middle of the corral. It looked like a gigantic dog with a thick brown mane running down its back.

Judging by its size, it had to weigh more than three hundred pounds and was squaring off with Duke, who looked like a lap dog in comparison.

Standing toe-to-toe, Duke bared his teeth and growled. The massive creature snarled back and hunched its shoulders.

Before Josie could yell for Duke to stand down, the two of them lunged at each other. Even though the larger animal was more powerful, Duke was faster on his feet and got the first lick in and bit the vicious creature in the shoulder. The creature snapped its jaws, but got only air. Duke cut around and went to bite the animal in the flank.

The bigger animal reared around and raked Duke's thigh with its razor-sharp talons.

Duke yelped and fell back on his rump.

The bloodthirsty creature went in for the kill.

Josie fired the shotgun and hit the thing in the front leg.

It roared with pain and glared at Josie.

The creature came at her. She had no time to pop out the spent shell and reload, so she turned and bolted straight out the gate, yelling for Duke to follow her.

She raced for the closest form of cover—her truck.

But when she ran around the back bumper, her hand banged into the open tailgate hanging on the chains, and she dropped the shotgun.

She dashed for the driver door, opened it, jumped in, and slammed it shut.

The creature stood up on its hind legs and hammered the side of the cab with its massive front paws.

Josie saw Duke lumbering for the truck. She slid across the bench seat, opened the passenger door. Duke leapt up and landed on the seat.

The creature scrambled around the front of the truck.

Josie swiftly closed the door. She squeezed around Duke and got behind the wheel.

The beast slammed against the door, its wild face just outside the window. Duke snarled and barked, pressing his muzzle up against the glass.

Josie reached up and flipped the sun visor down. The ignition key dropped in her palm. She started the engine and put the truck in gear.

She spun the truck around in the yard and steered for the driveway.

The truck shook like a falling boulder from an avalanche had hit it.

Josie glanced in the rearview mirror and saw the monstrous creature staring at her through the back window of the cab. It raised a gigantic paw and smashed the glass.

Before it could reach in with its deadly talons, Josie cranked the wheel, slamming the side of the truck into a big tree. The impact threw her and Duke across the cab and catapulted the creature out of the bed of the truck.

Josie sat up. The truck was still running, so she pulled away from the tree. She glanced in her side mirror and saw the creature lying on the ground, temporarily stunned, struggling to its feet.

Josie put the transmission into reverse, looked over her shoulder through the rear window, and trounced on the accelerator pedal. The truck raced backwards.

The creature looked up just as the lowered tailgate hit it like a guillotine blade and the back of the truck crashed against another tree.

Josie leaned forward on the steering wheel, shaken from the sudden jolt. She looked over at Duke. He'd been thrown against the dashboard and fallen onto the floorboard. He put his front paws on the seat and looked up at Josie.

"Sorry about that," she apologized.

She pulled up and turned the truck around so she could get a better look at the creature from the driver window and make sure it was dead.

Even with most of its head sheared off by the tailgate, it was an incredible creature to behold.

She remembered the stories her grandmother used to tell her when she was a child. Mountain folklore passed down through the generations. Her favorite had been about a gentle giant that was the guardian of the forest, protecting the other animals and the neighboring mountainfolk.

And like all tales, there was the scary one about the evil beasts that roamed the woods at night. Her grandmother called them bear-dogs. Josie recalled seeing illustrated pictures in an old book depicting the creatures—which looked much like the one she had just killed—hunting and eating farmers' sheep.

She had no idea they could really exist.

"Come on, let's get you back home and patch you up," Josie said, seeing the nasty wound on Duke's thigh.

But before she could put the truck into gear, Duke jumped up onto the bench seat. He glared out the windshield and growled.

"Now what?" Josie said.

She saw two bear-dogs running through the woods in the direction of the Pike farm.

"Oh my God," Josie said, and gunned the engine.

36

Having completed two major projects—painting the living room and building the chicken coop—Marcus decided he better organize the barn. The workbench was cluttered with paint cans and used paintbrushes he had to dispose of or put back on the shelves, along with tools that needed to be properly stowed away on the pegboard or placed back in drawers.

Josie had been overly generous giving him more building material than he really needed to erect the chickens' new home. He'd sorted through all of the wood planks, selecting the prime pieces that didn't have too many knots, as he knew in time the gnarly defects would fall out leaving gaping holes in his work. The bad pieces he'd tossed haphazardly into the back of the barn, creating an unsightly mess.

He heard a crackling popping noise and looked up just as the bulb went out in the light fixture mounted on an overhead rafter. The interior of the building went dark except for the sliver of daylight shining between the crack in the partially opened barn door.

Marcus also noticed a ray of light at the back of the barn, which he thought odd, as he had boarded up the rear side door. He walked over to the workbench and grabbed a flashlight but when he went to switch it on it didn't work. He unscrewed the end cap and dumped the batteries onto the bench. Right away he could smell the leaky batteries and knew they had corroded. He scooped up the batteries with a rag and dropped them into an empty paint can and tossed the useless flashlight in as well as he figured the contacts were probably ruined.

He went to the back of the barn and stepped around the partition by the stalls and was surprised to see the door pushed in and the crossbeam boards pried off the walls. The edges around the door were splintered. A crack ran down the center as if impacted by a battering ram.

"Great, another project." Marcus looked in the rear stall and saw an accumulation of more fish bones and crushed berries mingled in the hay on the dirt floor.

The front door of the barn creaked open.

Marcus turned and went around the partition expecting to see Libby or Kaylee entering the barn.

Instead he saw the dark silhouette of an enormous animal standing on four legs before the backdrop of brilliant sunlight.

The massive creature stepped into the barn.

Its features became better defined with each step.

It was some kind of giant dog.

Marcus' first reaction was a laboratory experiment gone terribly wrong, the way the muscles in the shoulders and legs bulged ready to rip out of the flesh.

The body was like a Bull Mastiff on steroids, but the face looked nothing like the breed. The head was huge with eyes set high on the forehead, a long broad snout, large nostrils—and vicious sharp teeth.

To add to its menacing look, the creature had a thick flank of hair running midway down its spine much like the flared headdress on a Roman helmet.

White vapor snorted out its nostrils.

Its beady eyes narrowed as it glared at Marcus.

Marcus took a step back and bumped into something that hadn't been there a few seconds ago. Whatever it was had crept up silently behind him.

He felt something heavy on his shoulder. It was a giant fur-covered hand with black, leathery knuckles, and yellowish-brown fingernails with chipped cuticles.

What now? It's not bad enough I'm being stalked by an abomination straight out of hell; some gorilla has to escape from a zoo and find its way into our barn. Aren't I one lucky bastard.

Marcus knew he had to look back—stare death in the face. He turned his head and saw a solid wall of fur. He craned his neck to look up. He had to, if he wanted to see its face. It had to be eight feet tall. He had never seen one before and always thought they were a hoax, but not anymore.

The Bigfoot looked down at him without expression as if it were studying a mushroom on the ground and was contemplating whether or not to eat it.

"Are you kidding me?"

Marcus heard a rumbling growl, turned, and was alarmed to see how close the other creature had advanced, standing less than ten feet away.

Before Marcus could react, the big hand on his shoulder pushed him firmly aside so that he had to catch himself before hitting the wall.

A dismissive shove, but not hostile.

Protective.

Marcus stood against the wall and watched as the six hundred pound Bigfoot faced off with the formative three hundred pound science project. The creature lunged up and slammed into the Bigfoot, sharp claws raking its chest.

Spinning around, the Bigfoot grabbed the giant creature by the throat and a front leg and swung it against the barn wall. The monstrous beast slid down, landed on its back, and scrambled to get up.

The Bigfoot picked up a four-foot long section of a 2 x 4 inch board.

The four-legged monster growled and charged a second time. Only the Bigfoot was ready and swung the board, clobbering the creature across the head and snapping the stud in two.

Again, the creature went down. When it regained its senses, it decided to choose an easier adversary and went for Marcus. The Bigfoot tried to grab the creature by a hind leg, but it was too fast and slipped through its fingers.

Marcus had nowhere to go so he jumped up on the workbench hoping to gain some advantage. When the creature got close enough, he began kicking paint cans off the tabletop, each one striking the animal in the face. It was enough of a distraction to give Marcus the opportunity to arm himself with a real weapon. He snatched the nail gun he had used to put up the plywood walls on the chicken coop and pointed it at the creature.

He pressed the trigger and fired off a short burst.

The 2 1/4 inch long nails struck the creature in the face. It came to a halt and yowled with pain, even pawing at its face to dislodge the tiny spikes.

The Bigfoot lumbered over and smashed its fist down on the massive animal's back, buckling its legs, and driving it to the ground.

But the muscular creature wasn't quite yet defeated and clambered back on its feet. It snapped its jaws and clamped down on the Bigfoot's right forearm.

This time it was the Bigfoot that roared with pain. With the collective force of a couple heavyweight-boxing champions, it punched the creature in the face, which turned out to be a bad mistake as one of the nail heads drove into the Bigfoot's knuckle. It pulled its fist free and held up its bloody hand and let out a wailing cry.

The dog-like creature released the Bigfoot's arm and stumbled away toward the front of the barn, making its escape.

Marcus fired off more nails but the thing was out of range. He emptied the feed and the gun quit.

The Bigfoot loped out of the barn after the creature.

Marcus rushed to the doorway.

The creature was running in the direction of the burn pile, but then suddenly stopped. It raised its head, sniffed the air, and then bolted in the other direction toward the house.

The Bigfoot was watching the creature cut diagonally across the field. It looked down at the ground and spotted some cobblestones that Marcus had gathered and put in a pile.

Bending down, the Bigfoot picked up a round rock the size of a grapefruit and hefted it in its giant hand, testing its weight.

Marcus stood by and watched as the Bigfoot cocked its arm. It stood back on one foot and pivoted, lining up the throw, like a quarterback giving his receiver enough lead before nailing the pass.

The creature galloped across the field.

The Bigfoot extended its arm and threw the rock with the intensity of a fired cannonball.

Marcus wouldn't have believed it if he hadn't seen it with his own eyes.

The trajectory was perfect and the rock struck the creature square in the side of the face.

Marcus ran after the Bigfoot to the massive animal lying dead in the snow. He couldn't believe the damage the cobblestone had caused.

The Bigfoot wasn't taking any chances. It picked up the same, now bloody rock, and pulverized the rest of the skull.

Marcus looked at the Bigfoot, unsure of what he should do next; if he was to become its next victim. Should he run? And if he did, would it chase him down and give him the same treatment and bash in his brains?

The Bigfoot gazed down at him then turned to the sound of an engine coming down the tree-lined drive.

It was Josie in her truck.

37

The first thing Josie saw as she pulled up was the tall hairy creature standing in the field with Marcus. All this time she'd doubted Avery when he tried to warn her about the Bigfoot.

But there it was, next to Marcus; like two neighbors discussing the weather.

Josie felt stupid for disbelieving Avery and treating him so poorly. She knew he had feelings for her. Known it for some time. Deep down, she did too. But she missed Lewis and her heart still ached for him. She knew the healing process would take some time before she could truly move on.

Josie turned off the engine. She climbed out and waved to Marcus.

He waved back and started walking toward the truck. The Bigfoot remained standing in the field.

Even though Duke was hurt, he still jumped down to stand by her side.

"Is everything all right?" Josie asked.

"It is now," Marcus replied. "Thanks to our friend back there."

Josie looked at the Bigfoot and could see something lying by its feet. "Is that a bear-dog?"

"Is that what you call it? Yeah. The Bigfoot killed it with a supersonic pitch if you can believe that."

"Where's the other one?" Josie asked, unable to disguise the worry in her voice.

"What other one? You mean there's more?"

"I killed one at my place. I saw two head over here."

Josie heard crashing glass. She turned and saw a bear-dog smash its way through the front window into Marcus' house.

"Oh my God, Libby and Kaylee!" Marcus yelled.

They were about to run for the house when they heard what sounded like a stampeding elephant. It was the Bigfoot, stomping into the yard.

The Bigfoot charged past the truck.

Duke didn't bark. Instead, he stared with bewilderment as though the Bigfoot was nothing more than a butterfly fluttering by.

Josie and Marcus jumped out of its way as it barreled through and lumbered up the porch steps.

Marcus groaned when the Bigfoot smashed through the front door.

Josie followed Marcus onto the porch. That's when she heard Kaylee scream.

They rushed to the gaping doorway and glanced inside.

The bear-dog had Libby and Kaylee cornered in the kitchen. Libby wielded a butcher knife and was standing in front of Kaylee to protect her daughter. Every time the monstrous creature took a step, Libby lashed out with the knife, forcing it back.

The Bigfoot roared and pounced on the bear-dog. The two creatures rolled on the floor, knocking over furniture and breaking everything under their massive bodies. The Bigfoot grappled with the bear-dog, trying to get it in a wrestler's hold and pin it to the floor, but each time it tried, the other animal would claw its way free or chomp down with a savage bite.

"Libby!" Marcus yelled, his voice barely audible in the din of the roaring Bigfoot and the snarling bear-dog. He moved along the wall staying clear of the skirmish and skirted over to the kitchen. "Come on, hurry," he shouted.

Libby grabbed his extended hand.

Kaylee clung to her mother and the three made their way around the room to the front door.

"Go wait by the truck," Marcus said. Libby picked Kaylee up in her arms and ran onto the porch.

Josie watched in amazement as the ferocious creatures fought. The bear-dog had the tenacity of a pit bull and refused to give up, lashing out with its claws as it squirmed under the burly Bigfoot.

She could tell by the expression on Marcus' face that he wanted to yell and tell them to get out, watching everything destroyed and all his hard work ruined by the two monstrous creatures, their blood splattering the freshly painted walls.

The Bigfoot grabbed a leg that had broken off the coffee table, lying on the floor.

It made for the perfect weapon as it had a jagged edge, so the Bigfoot used the pointy piece of wood and stabbed the bear-dog through the eye.

A piercing howl echoed in the house.

The Bigfoot shoved the shaft deeper into the bear-dog's brain.

Pushing the dead animal aside, the Bigfoot stood. It kicked the bear-dog a couple times with his huge foot to make sure it was dead. Then it turned and shambled out of the house.

Josie and Marcus kept a safe distance and followed the Bigfoot down the porch steps.

Everyone by the truck watched in awe as the Bigfoot ambled toward them. Its face and body were covered in blood, most of it the bear-dog's though the Bigfoot had suffered greatly and had cuts about its face and gashes all over its body.

Libby had put Kaylee down and she was standing next to her mother. Kaylee gazed up at the towering creature and said, "Hi."

The Bigfoot looked down at the little girl. It huffed and strode off.

Josie and the others watched the Bigfoot cross the field and disappear into the trees.

Kaylee went over to Marcus and peered up at her father. "See, Daddy. I told you there was a monster."

38

"How are you feeling?" Kate asked, sitting in the stiff plastic chair next to Cole's hospital bed. She was wearing a blue robe and slippers as the emergency doctor had insisted she be admitted for observation.

Cole turned his head and grinned. He held up his hand and showed her the pushbutton for self administering his pain medication. "Wonderful."

"While they were stitching you up, a sheriff's deputy got my statement."

"Really? What did you tell him?"

"Pretty much what happened."

"Pretty much?"

"Well, not everything. I told him we got lost in the snow and those men were trying to kill us."

Cole glanced over at the closed door and turned to Kate. "What about the claim?"

Kate shook her head.

"You never mentioned the gold?"

"No."

"Good. Uh-oh," Cole grimaced, raising his head off the pillow. He pressed his thumb on the pain dispenser. He laid his head back down and closed his eyes for a second, then opened them. "How long before they release me?"

"Doctor says it will be a few days. I'm sure there will be an investigation seeing as the sheriff was shot."

"How is he?"

"They had him in surgery. Nurse told me he's doing fine."

"Then I guess we're heroes."

"Looks that way."

***

Josie walked down the corridor and paused at the open doorway of the hospital room. The curtains were open. She could see a small patch of blue sky out the window indicating a break in the storm. She stepped into the room and placed the vase of flowers she had purchased from the gift shop on the table next to Avery's bed.

"Hi there," he said, opening his eyes.

"Seems I owe you an apology," Josie said, resting her hands on the side railing of the bed.

"Oh?"

Josie told him about the Bigfoot and how the noble creature had saved the Pike family from the bear-dogs.

"Bear-dogs?"

"That's what I said."

Avery smiled. "Tell me you're just humoring me."

"I'm dead serious."

The smile slowly faded. "Jesus. And all this time..."

Josie looked at the cuts on Avery's face, his bandaged legs, and the tube draining fluid out of his side into a bag attached to the lower railing of the bed. "My God, Avery."

"It's not as bad as it looks," Avery quipped, but it was obvious he was in some degree of pain.

Josie heard a rustling on the other side of the bed. "What's that?"

"Come around and see," Avery said.

When Josie stepped around the foot of the bed, she saw a dog curled up in the corner. "Who do we have here?"

"She's my rescue. One of the orderlies was nice enough to clean her up and get her some food from the cafeteria. Apparently she's particularly fond of barbeque spare ribs."

"Does she have a name?"

"Not yet. Any suggestions?"

Josie stepped closer. She offered her hand and the dog sniffed it. The dog lowered its head and allowed Josie to rub behind its ears. "She so sweet."

"You know, Josie. I've been wanting to talk to you about something. I know it's probably too soon, but—"

Josie stopped him by saying, "We'll have plenty of time to talk later. Right now, we have to decide what we're going to call this precious girl."

"Okay," Avery said.

"How about...Duchess?"

"You mean like Duchess and Duke?"

"Yes. What do you think?"

"I think that's a fine name."

39

Lou used the loader on the front of his tractor and excavated a burial pit deep enough to accommodate all of the dead sheep. He made sure the bottom was hard shale so there wouldn't be any threat of seepage into the underground water table and the trough was nowhere near the source for their well.

Usually, he only had to deal with a single dead animal and would place the carcass in a compost bin where the biodegradation process would decompose the organic material.

But as there were so many dead sheep, Lou decided it would be better to incinerate the corpses. He thought of contacting a rendering service that would come out and pick up the dead livestock, but then he would have to explain the strange creature he had found in the woods left by the Bigfoot. Instead of leaving it for the scavengers, Lou thought it would be best to include it with the sheep. The last thing he wanted was to attract other predators, especially ones like the one in the pit.

Besides, Arlene wasn't comfortable knowing it was out there even though it was dead.

Lou used his tractor and brought over tree branches and other combustible debris and dumped them into the burial pit, covering the bodies.

He walked around the rim and splashed gasoline, emptying a five-gallon can. He lit a roadside flare and tossed the fiery torch into the mass grave.

Backing away from the intense heat, Lou went over to the tractor and climbed up on the seat. He watched the fire build up. The flames shot up in the air in a loud *whoosh* as the billowing smoke rose in the sky. He could feel the hotness on his face and smell the terrible stench of burning wool and flesh.

He sat on the tractor for over an hour until the fire died down and the smoke had cleared and there were only charred skeletal remains.

Lou took that as his cue and started up the tractor. He scooped up piles of dirt he had dug up out of the hole and dumped them back into the smoldering trench.

After covering the hole, he patted the dirt down with the underside of the loader to flatten the ground.

He drove back to the farm and parked next to the shearing shed.

When he walked inside Arlene was standing next to the small enclosure. She turned and gave him a smile. "Come see."

As he approached he saw a ewe that had just given birth.

A newborn lamb—lubricated and still wet from the ruptured water bag—stood on shaky legs. The infant staggered for a bit then dipped its head under its mother's belly, and proceeded to nurse.

"I'd say we have ourselves a healthy lamb," Lou said proudly, thankful that it hadn't been a stillborn. Even after all that had happened and their tragic losses, Lou couldn't help thinking that the crisis was over and this was a new beginning.

"We have four other pregnant ewes that will be due shortly," Arlene boasted.

"That's great. This keeps up we'll have our flock back in no time."

"Best to keep our fingers crossed. Pass me that towel."

Lou grabbed the towel draped over the top rail and gave it to Arlene as she stepped into the pen.

Arlene knelt beside the lamb and dried its body off. She gave it a hug. "Welcome to your new home."

The lamb answered her back with a long shrill bleat.

"Guess the feeling's mutual," Lou said and they both laughed.

40

Marcus stood a few feet away from the bonfire and watched the flames. There was little threat of the fire spreading with the snow on the ground though Marcus had to keep track of the embers floating in the air, making sure they didn't travel too far and end up in the trees. He had four buckets of water close by if he needed to douse the fire.

He hadn't mentioned to the fire marshal there would be animal carcasses buried under all the busted up furniture and rubbish when he secured his fire permit for the burn pile, which probably explained the smell and why the fire was crackling so much.

Marcus had also tossed in the damaged barn door. He had decided not to hang another door and leave the entrance in the back of the barn open for whenever the Bigfoot wanted to pay a visit to the stall. He had spruced the nook up with some fresh hay and gone to the trouble of leaving some berries in a bowl.

Libby and Kaylee came out of the house and walked across the field toward the roaring fire.

"Ooh, that's stinky," Kaylee said and took a step back, holding her nose.

The morning breeze shifted and the smoke blew in their direction.

"We better get back," Libby said, grabbing Kaylee's hand and moving away as they fanned the smoke out of their faces.

"Sorry about that," Marcus apologized.

"How about we take a little walk?" Libby said to Kaylee.

"Okay. Is Daddy coming?"

"I have to stay here," Marcus said. "Watch the fire. You two go."

Kaylee looked up at Libby. "Can Bunny come?"

"Sure, as long as you carry her. I don't want her running off."

"Thanks, Mom." Kaylee dashed over to the chicken coop.

Libby turned and faced Marcus. "Josie said she has some old furniture she's been storing in her barn that she's been meaning to get rid of."

"Some old furniture, huh? Probably more like keepsakes."

"What should I tell her?"

Marcus gazed at the fire. "Well, seeing as our stuff is going up in smoke, we might as well accept."

"Mom! We're ready!" Kaylee called out, holding her pet chicken in her arms.

"Okay, I'll be right there!" Libby yelled. She turned to Marcus. "When we come back, I'll help you with some of the repainting then we can go over to Josie's."

"Sounds good," Marcus said and went back to monitoring the bonfire.

When Libby turned, she realized Kaylee had already gone. She went over and saw her daughter's footprints in the snow and followed them into the woods.

"Kaylee!" she shouted. "Wait for Mom!"

It was impossible to tell if she was even on the path. As Libby trekked through the snow she called out again. She started to worry when there was no reply. Kaylee was nowhere to be seen. *How could she have gotten so far ahead?*

Libby picked up the pace and slogged across the snow. "Kaylee! Where are you?"

Finally, Kaylee answered, "I'm over here!"

Trudging through the trees, Libby saw Kaylee standing by the creek beside a large snow-covered rock with a tiny blue object on top. "Honey, didn't you hear me calling?"

"Look Mom," Kaylee said, pointing. "The monster gave me back Bunny's egg."

Libby stared at the egg. "Are you sure you didn't—"

And then she heard the branches rustling across the stream.

She looked across the narrow span of water and saw the Bigfoot watching them.

Libby glanced down at Kaylee, but her daughter was preoccupied with the egg and hadn't noticed the creature in the forest.

When Libby gazed up, the Bigfoot was gone. She couldn't explain it, but it was comforting knowing it was out there.

"What should we do with it?" Kaylee asked, as Bunny fidgeted in her arms.

Libby scooped up the egg and placed it gingerly in her coat pocket. "You can have it for breakfast. Tomorrow, we'll bring a fresh one."

"So, he's not *really* a monster, is he?"

"No, honey. He's our friend."

Kaylee smiled up at her mother. Libby grinned and they walked home.

THE END

ACKNOWLEDGEMENTS

    I would like to thank Gary Lucas and the wonderful people working with Severed Press that helped with this book. Special thanks to Nichola Meaburn for her editing and keen eye. It's truly amazing how folks we may never meet and who live in the most incredible places in the world can truly enrich our lives. I would especially like to thank my daughter and faithful beta reader, Genene Griffiths Ortiz, for making this so much fun and sharing these bizarre and incredible journeys.

ABOUT THE AUTHOR

Gerry Griffiths lives in San Jose, California, with his family and their five rescue dogs and a cat. He is a Horror Writers Association member and has over thirty published short stories in various anthologies and magazines, as well as a short story collection entitled *Creatures*. He is also the author of *Silurid*, *The Beasts of Stoneclad Mountain*, and *Down From Beast Mountain* as well as *Death Crawlers* with the follow-up standalone novels, *Deep in the Jungle*, *The Next World*, and *Battleground Earth,* all published by Severed Press.

SEVEREDPRESS

facebook.com/severedpress
twitter.com/severedpress

CHECK OUT OTHER GREAT HORROR NOVELS

MONSTROSITY
by Tim Curran

The Food. It seeped from the ground, a living, gushing, teratogenic nightmare. It contaminated anything that ate it, causing nature to run wild with horrible mutations, creating massive monstrosities that roam the land destroying towns and cities, feeding on livestock and human beings and one another. Now Frank Bowman, an ordinary farmer with no military skills, must get his children to safety. And that will mean a trip through the contaminated zone of monsters, madmen, and The Food itself. Only a fool would attempt it. Or a man with a mission.

THE SQUIRMING
by Jack Hamlyn

You are their hosts.

You are their food.

The parasites came out of nowhere, squirming horrors that enslaved the human race. They turned the population into mindless pack animals, psychotic cannibalistic hordes whose only purpose was to feed them.

Now with the human race teetering at the edge of extinction, extermination teams are fighting back, killing off the parasites and their voracious hosts. Taking them out one by one in violent, bloody encounters.

The future of mankind is at stake.

And time is running out.

SEVEREDPRESS

facebook.com/severedpress
twitter.com/severedpress

CHECK OUT OTHER GREAT HORROR NOVELS

BLACK FRIDAY
by Michael Hodges

Jared the kleptomaniac, Chike the unemployed IT guy, Patricia the shopaholic, and Jeff the meth dealer are trapped inside a Chicago supermall on Black Friday. Bridgefield Mall empties during a fire alarm, and most of the shoppers drive off into a strange mist surrounding the mall parking lot. They never return. Chike and his group try calling friends and family, but their smart phones won't work, not even Twitter. As the mist creeps closer, the mall lights flicker and surge. Bulbs shatter and spray glass into the air. Unsettling noises are heard from within the mist, as the meth dealer becomes unhinged and hunts the group within the mall. Cornered by the mist, and hunted from within, Chike and the survivors must fight for their lives while solving the mystery of what happened to Bridgefield Mall. Sometimes, a good sale just isn't worth it.

GRIMWEAVE
by Tim Curran

In the deepest, darkest jungles of Indochina, an ancient evil is waiting in a forgotten, primeval valley. It is patient, monstrous, and bloodthirsty. Perfectly adapted to its hot, steaming environment, it strikes silent and stealthy, it chosen prey: human. Now Michael Spiers, a Marine sniper, the only survivor of a previous encounter with the beast, is going after it again. Against his better judgement, he is made part of a Marine Force Recon team that will hunt it down and destroy it.

The hunters are about to become the hunted.

SEVEREDPRESS

facebook.com/severedpress
twitter.com/severedpress

CHECK OUT OTHER GREAT HORROR NOVELS

DEATH CRAWLERS
by Gerry Griffiths

Worldwide, there are thought to be 8,000 species of centipede, of which, only 3,000 have been scientifically recorded. The venom of Scolopendra gigantea—the largest of the arthropod genus found in the Amazon rainforest—is so potent that it is fatal to small animals and toxic to humans. But when a cargo plane departs the Amazon region and crashes inside a national park in the United States, much larger and deadlier creatures escape the wreckage to roam wild, reproducing at an astounding rate. Entomologist, Frank Travis solicits small town sheriff Wanda Rafferty's help and together they investigate the crash site. But as a rash of gruesome deaths befalls the townsfolk of Prospect, Frank and Wanda will soon discover how vicious and cunning these new breed of predators can be. Meanwhile, Jake and Nora Carver, and another backpacking couple, are venturing up into the mountainous terrain of the park. If only they knew their fun-filled weekend is about to become a living nightmare.

THE PULLER
by Michael Hodges

Matt Kearns has two choices: fight or hide. The creature in the orchard took the rest. Three days ago, he arrived at his favorite place in the world, a remote shack in Michigan's Upper Peninsula. The plan was to mourn his father's death and figure out his life. Now he's fighting for it. An invisible creature has him trapped. Every time Matt tries to flee, he's dragged backwards by an unseen force. Alone and with no hope of rescue, Matt must escape the Puller's reach. But how do you free yourself from something you cannot see?

Printed in Germany
by Amazon Distribution
GmbH, Leipzig